THE
MUSEUM
OF
BULLSHIT

A NOVEL
BY **BRAD RAU**

—SmallPub—

for my father

"*Well now, you'll be amazed when I tell you that I'm sure that they exist....Well, I'm a romantic, so I always wanted them to exist....Of course, the big, big criticism of all this is, 'Where is the body?' You know, why isn't there a body? I can't answer that, and maybe they don't exist, but I want them to.*"

—Dr. Jane Goodall

(Talk of the Nation, 9/27/2002)

THE APPOINTMENT BEGAN amiably, as Louis had anticipated. Auster was cordial, warm. Even for her evident impatience, so was Lydia.

There seemed no reason for it to be otherwise; nothing but common ground here. Hell, Louis thought, to look at the pair, they could have been siblings; pale faces framed with gray. Her hair: short and styled so that it could be carelessly kept. Long and kept carelessly, his was tied back in a snarl. Even their clothes seemed somehow uniform. Old fabric, vibrant colors and elastic cuffs exhausted; the cumulative effect exclaiming to the world, "I'm not naked, and so have fulfilled any obligations to decent society." Their taste in clothing was congruent. Their vocations, parallel.

After leading Louis and Lydia into his office, Marcus Auster made a big production of shaking the rain from his coat before hanging it on the coat-tree by the door. Louis immediately understood the act as performance. Nothing much came off. It wasn't raining all that hard; misty out; the way it always is on this part of the Olympic Peninsula at this time of year. Outside, a gunmetal gelatin held the trees apart and kept the heavy sky from collapsing and smothering them all.

Inside, Marcus Auster's office was warm and lit in tobacco-stain hues. On the bookcases around the room, old tomes were held apart by curios in glass jars. Teetering piles of paper drooped over the edges of the shelves, like frozen waterfalls. The walls hosted framed photos of men posing next to impossible creatures: a squid dangling thirty feet long, held aloft by the arm of a crane, a snake held up by twenty-some men, shoulder to shoulder.

Before taking his seat behind the desk, Marcus shook Lydia's hand, welcoming her. He wasted a moment, pontificating about what a pleasure it was, lamenting it hadn't happened sooner.

And then he shook Louis's hand.

The curator's paw was fever-hot and dry, the skin swollen around his wedding band. In his hesitant greeting was an unasked question: why was Louis here? Who was Louis at all? The man smiled too softly—a reflexive acknowledgement that he could see Louis as a black man; that he recognized the racisms of the world; that he did not consider himself party to them. Which was bullshit, Louis thought. He, just like every other American, owned racism—whether or not it was an endowment they desired.

For her part, Lydia provided no explanation for Louis's presence. Neither did Louis. Then, when they'd all sat and settled, and Louis asked if Marcus would mind him recording, it seemed to resolve itself in the museum curator's mind: Louis was a reporter.

It might not have been technically accurate, but that was clearly the conclusion the curator came to.

With a dainty sweep of his hand, suddenly pleased that someone from the media was along, Auster announced, "Of course," his tone brimming with welcoming pride. In the next moment, his attention settled back on Lydia.

As Louis would have guessed, the meeting began with talk of the Wilton Incident. Where else would it have? Everything seemed to begin there. All of Lydia's work—the thick books, the thin ones, the articles published in dubious scientific journals—seemed to begin or culminate there.

"It's really a wonder we haven't met before now," Marcus mused aloud for the second time. "It's really quite remarkable. I grew up just outside of Wilton. A shame about Michael. You have my condolences."

Lydia had no response for that. Not a verbal one. The corners of her mouth turned down.

Auster continued, "I did meet him once or twice, you know? At conferences and the like. A remarkable man."

Louis could feel Lydia's gaze graze him for just a moment. By the time he turned to her, she was already looking Auster's way again. Her impatience could be read in every spasm of her hand, in the patter of her tapping foot. "The specimen... I'm sorry, I'm sure you understand," she scratched behind her ear with the sudden ferocity of a cat attending to a flea bite, then combed her hair back into place with the very fingers which had upset it. "I'm quite anxious to see it. As you can imagine, I have a lot of questions," she gave a little pause, pushing back the mounds of paper on the desk's edge, clearing a little place where she leaned her wrists. It was like she'd taken ownership of the whole desktop with that one gesture. "First of all, where exactly was it found?"

"Well," Marcus puffed. His eyelid twitched. "I can only say that it was found nearby." He gestured broadly, padding time. "On the Peninsula, I mean to say."

Lydia glowered. "You won't tell me where it was found?"

The underside of the curator's eyelid quivered again. "I cannot."

"Cannot?"

Marcus Auster shook his head. "I'm afraid not, no."

"And the men who found it?"

The curator shook his head more woefully. The room was quiet.

In the silence, Louis penned notes on the pad in his hand. The felt tip made a fervent, unintelligible whisper on the paper. Louis took notes even with his phone set, recording everything. His notes detailed the curator's office. He wrote down every impression that the microphone could not capture. He wrote down everything even though all of it accorded with his expectations (the photos, the curios, the unkempt piles of paper).

"I can't speak with with them?"

"As part of the museum's contract to host the exhibit there are, naturally, clauses of anonymity. I'm sorry, but I'm sure you understand."

"I don't."

"It could be dangerous for them. Hunters, in this day and age, are rarely embraced by our culture at large. Especially when the trophy is this remarkable."

Lydia's voice rose a notch, her words turning abrupt. She wasn't shouting, but it seemed to Louis she was on a short path there. "You're claiming your museum has the greatest zoological find of the last two centuries and I can't even know the names of the men who..."

Marcus raised a finger to correct her. "The greatest *cryptozoological* find in two centuries."

Inhaling deeply, Lydia pulled back and when she leaned forward again, she said, "That term, I'm sure you are aware, describes that which is unsubstantiated, Mr. Auster. If you're claiming, what you have here is verifiable..."

"Please, call me Marcus. I'm sorry. Yes. You're right, of course. I assure you, this is legitimate. Bona fide, as they say. It's just... Well, to put it bluntly, cryptozoology is the museum's brand. Even after verification I, personally, would still call it a cryptid. For marketing and... We wouldn't want the Smithsonian swooping in..." The man laughed.

Lydia did not. "I didn't come here to talk about branding."

The man forced a smile onto his face. "I know, I know... Such matters must seem trifling to a scientific mind like yours. But, here at the museum..."

She stood abruptly and Marcus Auster seemed dumbfounded by it. Staring up at her for a moment, his eye lid quivered more conspicuously.

"I'd think you'd at least reserve your judgement until after you've seen it."

"Let's see it, then."

Swiping his phone from the desktop and sliding it into the inside pocket of his coat, Louis got to his feet as well. Marcus remained seated a moment longer.

"Fine," he said, still staring up at Lydia. "Well, then... Yes. Let's see it." He slapped the armrests of his chair and levered himself up. "Away we go."

He led them into the lobby.

Passing through a corral of rope stanchion and then through an imposing archway which, up close, looked as sketchy as stage setting, the threesome spilled into the museum proper—a long warehouse that had been divided into a winding pathway by segments of temporary wall.

Marcus led Lydia on, while Louis dropped to the rear of the pack.

Around him, strange artifacts cluttered the corners, and he tried to seal their impressions in his brain, and the words that might best illuminate those impressions. Beside an ornately carved mermaid meant to lead the bow of a ship, a gray, weathered thing was suspended in a glass case. It looked like something cobbled together from found bits of fish.

Behind the next insubstantial wall, a diorama had been assembled, displaying various 'breeds' of Jackalope (rabbits with antelope horns absurdly affixed to their craniums by some callous taxidermist). They sat, arranged as though grazing on a rise of plaster that had been doused with matte green paint.

A likeness of the Loch Ness monster stood beside the grainy photo on which it had been based. The resemblance was spot-on, but the lack of detail in the photo made both artifacts seem false.

Fairies floated in hunks of lucite. Tiny, imaginary prisoners.

lagomorph
cornibus

c. 1992

AT THE FAR END of the museum, a large area had been rearranged—the disorder of it still unresolved—to accommodate the museum's newest and most impressive specimen.

At over seven feet tall, the figure's shoulders and hips were too wide to be mistaken for human. The face seemed somehow inexact—deep wrinkles settling into implausible areas. Framed in tufts of fur, the skin of the cheeks and nose looked like it had been blacked with boot polish.

Arriving at the foot of the display, Auster announced proudly, "As you can see, we still have some final tweaking to do to layout of the exhibit, but..."

Lydia cut him short, "What about the insides? Who examined it before the taxidermy?"

Auster's grandiose tone withered. "It came this way, I'm afraid. Already prepared. A real loss, I agree."

Lydia stammered a moment. "Who did the work?"

"I couldn't say. The men who brought it in were insistent on sharing as little with me as possible—equally insistent I share even less. It's all in the contract, I'm afraid."

While he spoke, Lydia fished her phone out of her handbag, but before she could snap off the picture she'd framed, Auster hurried to get his hand atop the device, gently forcing it down. "I apologize, Ms. Swane. No photographs. The contract."

Seized by a sudden pain in his chest, Louis fell back into the shadows as Lydia's face puckered. "I'm confused, Mr. Auster. I thought I was invited here for my professional opinion: to make an assessment."

"Yes. Of course. And I'm terribly interested in hearing your thoughts. At the same time, you must understand... I can't have..." He shook his head. "There are postcards in the gift shop I'd be happy to provide you with..."

Continuing his slow retreat, one of the spotlights mounted on the ceiling caught Louis's eye: too bright. He was suddenly out of breath, drowning in the open air. Still back-stepping, falling deeper into the darkness beyond the spotlight's influence, the glassy eyes of the monster on the pedestal seemed to follow him.

"Postcards. Postcards? Are you being serious, Auster?"

"Call me Marcus, please," the man seemed to beg. "Yes, I am. Quite."

"Are you going to tell me I can't take a sample, either?"

"A sample?" The phrase came out with a note of disgust.

"For a DNA test..."

Still back pedaling, Louis slid into another shock of light, another electric shard sizzling in his chest. For just a moment he was transported. That young redhead, whose name he could not remember (so pale that every vein in her neck seemed as distinct as roads on a map) was in his face, dabbing his forehead with a round, soft bristled brush. Over the girl's shoulder, the producer's face appeared, a woman who's name he would not forget. "We like it Louis," she was saying, looking at her clipboard, as though reading script. Turning to him, she said, "But could you say honky, instead? That older demographic really responds to honky..."

He stumbled, one foot catching the other. Somehow, he succeeded in staying upright. His head felt like it was drifting away, the graceless fluidity of drunkenness infecting his every movement. He gasped. A thin rasp quaked in his throat. Still, barely a spoonful of air.

Reaching under his jacket, knocking the slim brick of his cellphone aside, where it hung loosely in his inside pocket, he clutched his chest.

He was having a heart attack.

That must be it. He dug his fingers in, pushing the tips into the sinewy gaps between the ribs, as though—maybe—he could get his heart going right again with just a little prodding.

In the glare of the spotlight, Marcus Auster was projecting, gesticulating with the lurching flamboyance of a silent film star. "Oh. Oh, no, no, no..." His eyelid trembled. "I am terribly sorry. We should have discussed all of this beforehand. I can't have... You seem to misunderstand the nature of the museum's stewardship of this particular artifact: it does not belong to the museum, it is simply on loan, you see, and so allowing you to molest it..."

"Molest? All I need are a few hairs..."

"But you understand, I can't grant permission for that. The proper owners..." The twitch in the man's eyelid seemed to have infected his whole face. For a brief moment, his cheeks spasmed and his jaw tightened and his nose wrinkled. "It simply isn't possible."

Lydia's tone had gone cold. "Look, if you were hoping I would come here and verify something that..."

Behind them, Louis had started huffing shallowly. To Lydia it sounded like he was scuffing his shoes on the floor. The noise nagged her patience, already ragged.

"Just look at it, Ms. Swane. How could you even doubt... Is the very sight of the beast which you've hunted for the past four decades not enough proof for you? I'm terribly sorry, I wouldn't have invited you here if I thought..."

"...If you thought I'd be skeptical? Scientific?"

The man turned to look up at the beast reverently. "How can you even question it? Seeing it, how can you question it at all? Seeing is believing, after all—isn't that the saying?"

"That maxim predates genetic sequencing, Mr. Auster. I'm interested in proof."

"In the pudding." The man gestured toward the display.

The shock and soft crack of the concrete floor meeting Louis's knee brought him back for a moment. He let loose a strained whimper. The spotlight above him was growing brighter somehow—flooding everything out. Louis was, certainly, already dead—floating off in a panic toward that spangled light.

But, the sound of him falling brought Lydia's attention around.

Hurrying to him, she managed to catch his shoulders before his head smacked the floor. Laying him out gently, she wrung herself around to face Marcus Auster, standing there dumbly.

"Call an ambulance," She barked, and then shouted after him, "Quickly!" when he lumbered away.

Turning back to Louis, she suddenly saw Michael's features in his face. They could have been father and son.

LYDIA WAS SILENT, glowering through the windscreen with such intensity it seemed a miracle the glass could withstand it. The wipers lunged back and forth, belching and squawking; the thick mist an inadequate lubricant. Still, it was too damp to navigate the road for more than a few breaths without them running.

By the time the paramedics had shown, the local police chief (a man named Conner) had already been on the scene for fifteen minutes, long enough to see Louis's attack subside. The chief hung around anyway, watching the goings on as though an opening for investigation might present itself. When Louis refused to get on the stretcher, the man's bushy eyebrows rose.

Instead, Louis was escorted to the ambulance by an EMT who hovered near his side, watching him, an upraised hand close, but not touching him, as though it was some telekinetic power animating Louis, and not Louis's own will. Conner followed silently, paces behind.

With Louis settled on the tailgate of the ambulance, the EMT asked if he had ever had a panic attack before. There was nothing wrong with him.

The episode concluded.

The EMTs closed up the ambulance and took to the road. Before packing himself off as well, the chief approached Lydia to tell her in a conspiratorial tone, "Don't let him drive."

Coming from Lydia's mouth, the advice was ignored. So now, that horrid gray finally drained from his face, Louis hunched rigidly behind the wheel.

Beyond the warm, arid heat blasting through Louis's sedan —the ultimate trophy of American success: a German automobile—the waterfront of Evany passed by, shuttered up, abandoned for the winter. The menacing, gray chop of Dabob Bay could be seen in snippets between the buildings. Two large restaurants, the windows of both covered over with plywood, were separated by a string of empty rental cabins and a souvenir shop with an overabundance of closed signs cluttering the windows.

The marina at the end of the queue was the most packed-up-looking property of them all: the docks pulled up and stacked at the water's edge; the parking lot cluttered with boats on risers, shrouded up in white like an assembly of antique Egyptian dead. Beyond the bay, a black curtain of rain had been drawn across the far shore. The other side of the road was only trees, Douglas Firs, stabbing toward the sky, clinging to a vertiginous incline.

Past the marina, Route 101 hitched away from the water and cut a swerving alley through the trees, up the slope. At the midpoint, tertiary roads began branching away from the thoroughfare. Though, to Louis's eyes, accustomed to the suspended highways tying knots around Seattle, there was nothing significant about this road at all. Nothing, other than that it reminded him of his childhood.

In the rearview, the bay dissolved into a gray monotony of sky and mist before the road settled out into the greater expanse of Evany.

Though the narrow waterfront below was what made the town a draw in the summertime—and that, what made it viable year round—this higher part of town was where everything civil sat: the town hall, the post office, supermarket, the tightly nestled neighborhoods. Even so, everything up here, to Louis's eyes, seemed somehow temporary. Maybe it was the emptiness of the streets, though certainly that was a result of the weather. The rain wasn't bad right now, but the wind was cold and hard against the side of the car, making steering a chore of constant correction. Maybe it was the fact that the sky had devoured the mountains behind the town and seemed so hungry to eat up anything else it could. Maybe it was the lingering decorations from the lapsed holiday season. The unlit trees in the storefronts brought Louis right back to the dismal Christmas he'd had three weeks past.

His mother had bought a house on the coast, south of Grayland. Every time he'd visited, the property had been ravaged by wind. Christmas was no exception.

It seemed to him an inhospitable place, and he could not fathom why his mother had chosen it.

Arriving in the dark, any view of the ocean was veiled by the nighttime but its noise was omnipresent. The crashing filled Louis ears like water after a dive. A heavy sound. A sound that could smother you. Louis had been slow, getting out of the car, full of a pointless dread, and Maria had taken his arm and leaned her head into his shoulder and hurried him up the path. The wind was too strong. It carried away the scent of her shampoo, a comfort he would have appreciated.

The windows of his mother's house were lit softly, the way the wax wall of a lit candle glows. In the bay window, Louis could see a tree, a spiny black bush, tacked with stars. Nothing about it made him want to be there any more. It was inexplicable. Louis loved his mother, for her every fault. He loved his fiancé in spite of her admirable but somehow annoying absence of faults and should have, by all accounts, wanted to be there with them. He should have wanted to be there more than anywhere else.

Inside, the walls shook with the wind, seemingly intent on coaxing an argument out of the family inside—Louis, his mother, and Maria. There was no one else. His grandfather had passed a decade ago, and even if the man had been alive, he wouldn't have been invited.

The wind blew.

The picture frames on the walls clattered. To talk, one had to yell. The strain of it dialed up Louis's nerves—all this having to yell to be heard, having to listen to someone yelling; his mother's insistent laugh—laughing so hard, just to make it heard. Louis had snapped at her, his sour mood spilling out into the room.

The next day, Christmas proper, the wind was even worse. The power went out. The tree looked disheartened with the lights unlit.

"Watch out for this light," Lydia said, bringing Louis back to the moment.

She was braced for impact and the tires squealed, sliding a few feet past the line where traffic was supposed to stop.

Exhaling, relaxing, Lydia eased back into her seat.

Louis cleared his throat. "My bad."

They passed a crew of municipal workers, taking down banners and strings of bulbs from the street lamps. Holiday cheer had crumbled, was being swept up and carted away. All that was left ahead was the cold, inhumane remainder of winter.

Normally, Louis wasn't bothered by it. Native to Washington state, he'd spent his adult life as a guest to the dreariness Puget Sound cultivates. But this Christmas had been particularly challenging (a first holiday for his mother and Maria) and seemed somehow culpable for the clouds, the rain, the cold. The heaviness of all of that, now seemed to have rooted itself inside him. New Years, that perennial, hollow vestige of hope had let him down so many times in his young adulthood that he'd learned to expect nothing from it at all.

This year it had culminated in an argument with Maria, which he only realized afterward he'd instigated and pursued even though there was no benefit for anyone in his doing so. It left him revolted with himself.

ACROSS FROM THE SUPERMARKET, so that it seemed the very center of town, the Evany Motel stood, the cinderblock face painted the color of banana flesh, the windows as dark as the wet pavement encircling it. When Louis settled his Benz beside Lydia's SUV—a Toyota 4Runner that looked like it had only occasionally spent time on pavement—Lydia unbuckled herself and hunched forward for the door handle. "Well, it was interesting spending the day with you, Louis. Take care of yourself."

"Wait," he said, stopping her from pulling the handle.

She didn't lean back, or let go of the door, but she did turn his way.

"That's it?"

Lydia shrugged. What else could there be?

"I mean..."

She repeated the gesture, a little more dismissively, a little quicker. "Hoaxes are pervasive... I warned you of that."

"You weren't even a little convinced, seeing it? It looked real, didn't it?" He felt uncertain. Wasn't he supposed to be the objective one?

"Of course. That's the whole point, Louis. If you're going to make a fake, you make it look real. Otherwise..." Finally, she let go of the door handle, but only to gesture—a motion implying null, emptiness.

"Yeah. But it did look real."

"He wouldn't let me take a picture."

Louis shrugged. "He did say that he didn't actually own the..." he nearly said *Bigfoot* but stopped himself. Bringing that word into the conversation would have made it all seem too entirely ludicrous. They were adults, both of them. And she was the one who was supposed to believe, and if she didn't... not even with what she'd seen...

Shaking her head, she said, "He keeps his museum dark because he doesn't want patrons seeing the seams, the falseness of everything. He doesn't want me taking pictures because he doesn't want any of it scrutinized. I'm sorry, Louis." Sighing, she finally relaxed, leaning back against the seat. "I'll tell you. He mentioned meeting Michael. Truth is, I have met Marcus Auster before. And if Michael were alive today, Auster wouldn't have invited us there. Auster, that man, is not a serious curator. He's not a serious researcher. He is not a serious anything."

Louis nodded and looked ahead.

"Well," she leaned forward again, hand on the handle once more. "Thanks for the ride. Please take care of yourself, Louis." She passed him a motherly glance before slipping out into the blustery parking lot.

Louis stayed in the driver's seat, watching the woman as she hurried under the Motel balcony and up the stairs. She disappeared into her room. Louis sat a moment longer.

THE MOMENT THE DAY DISSOLVED, the rain descended, a blitz of silver pins slashing through the night, clattering off the big window of Lydia's motel room.

She'd gotten a salad from the supermarket across the street. Standing before the shelves of wine, wavering for a long while, in the end, she'd picked a bottle of kombucha from an end-cap refrigerator, worrying wine would be a mistake. Her emotions still felt charged after the scare at the museum; she worried alcohol wouldn't help.

Sitting crosslegged on the hotel bed, staring at the TV without registering a thing she saw, she ate. An unhappy affair. The vibrant green of the lettuce belied a texture like soaked newspaper. Swallowing the last bite, she looked at the clock on the nightstand to find it was only a quarter past seven. The emptiness of the room seemed to swell.

Since Michael had passed, evenings were particularly difficult. They seemed somehow eternal, and the distractions of the day, the things that kept her hands busy, always felt inadequate when challenged with darkness.

She considered sneaking back across the street and finding a reasonably priced Malbec to keep her company, voted up the proposition, and was just tugging on her boots when a knock on the door interrupted her.

Louis stood on the balcony.

It was a surprise seeing him; Lydia'd already resigned herself to the fact that they would never meet again and now... Here he was, holding up a six pack of beer.

He looked different in this light.

She'd made the mistake of searching him online after getting back to the motel room. What she'd found tainted him. But, here he was, smiling and saving her a trip out in the rain. She shrugged, kicked off her boots and backed into the room, leaving the door wide.

"Were you headed out?"

Lydia shook her head.

When he took one of the round armchairs by the window, rather than taking the one opposite, Lydia backed up and took the chair at the desk. Popping open a can, he had to stretch out long to hand it to her, and she had to lean as well, to retrieve it. With the can between her thighs, she wiped the lip with the untucked tail of her shirt.

"My hands are clean," he said.

"The can isn't." After she'd swabbed the lip, she held the can out to toast, "To failed endeavors."

He screwed up his face, smiling eyes and a downturned mouth.

"No?"

He thumbed the tab on his beer can. It sang out a wavering, off-tune tone, a bit like the noise of the cheap Mbira thumb piano on his bookshelf back home. He said, "Seems premature."

"I won't be convinced to stay, if that's why you're here."

He raised his can and toasted, "How about, 'to truths'."

"Plural. Interesting." They both leaned in. She tapped her can against his—another off-tone Mbira note. They each took a sip. When Lydia pulled the can away from her mouth, she hesitated a moment before saying, "So, are you trying to tell me you and a honky might have separate truths."

Louis flinched. He covered it instantly with a smile. "You don't strike me as a Right World News sort..."

"Right World News doesn't strike me as news at all." She searched his face for a reaction and said, "You told me you were a writer. I've known a lot of writers in my life, not one who could afford a brand new Mercedes."

"It's entry level," he said. She looked him in the eye and Louis refused to look away.

"The Right World News wasn't what I expected to find."

Louis shrugged and said, "Brother's gotta make money," and he tipped his can her way, inviting her to another sip.

"Is that what you are: a brother?"

Now, he smirked and winked. "Only child. No siblings."

He drank longer than she did and so she got a chance to watch him, while his eyes were closed and his chin raised. She could no longer see any resemblance to Michael in him. Maybe that was a result of what the internet had shown her. It was hard reconciling this man with the rancor he'd spouted online. When he'd been lying on the museum floor, struggling to breath, he'd seemed like he could have been Michael's own child. Now, it was clear, all that united the men was the tone of their skin and the panic that had tightened her chest, watching someone who—she was certain—was dying.

After Louis had swallowed and opened his eyes, Lydia said, "Money, and that's all a man needs?"

"That doesn't have anything to do with why I'm here," Louis lied. It seemed to him Lydia could tell, and he hurried away from the subject. "But, you won't stay? You won't even consider it?"

Lydia shook her head.

"I'm surprised. You've been doing this, what?—nearly forty years now. I expected..."

"A zealot?" Even she wasn't certain whether she was being playful or provocative; the word had come out harsher than she'd intended. It didn't matter. Before he'd knocked on her door, she'd been convinced that she wouldn't ever see him again. That certainty had only been displaced by a few hours.

He snorted. "I guess. Something like that. Someone who would give the benefit of the doubt, at any rate. You don't feel Marcus Auster's new prize is even worth looking into? You're that convinced it's fake?"

Looking into the mouth of her can, Lydia let the question sit a moment. "Jane Goodall, you remember her?—famous zoologist..."

"You had an epigraph at the beginning of *The Wilton Incident: History and Hysteria*, attributed to her."

That he knew that, surprised her—stalled her for a moment. She frowned. "You know that one, huh?"

"I've read them all. Every one of them."

Lydia's frown deepened. "Maybe we oughta come clean with each other, Louis."

"Okay," he said and was quiet.

Lydia held the silence, thinking that he'd speak and when he didn't, she said, "Why did you track me down? Why did you want to be a part of this?"

"Well. It's a story and..."

"Louis, you're not a reporter. You lied to me about that," she said—there was a motherly warning to her tone—and it brought his attention up from where it had waned to the beer in his hand. When his gaze settled back on her, she said, "I told you, I looked you up. I saw what you do. You're not a reporter."

He tipped his empty hand. "I didn't say I was a reporter, I said I was a writer and..."

"And you made it seem like you were writing about this."

"I am. I have a book deal."

"To write about this?"

"So, I have a day job you don't think highly of. That precludes me from having an interest in Bigfoot?"

"You can have any interest you want." She took a long, slow breath and then hurried to say, "Michael wouldn't want anyone writing about him because he was black. Especially if..." She gestured and let the statement die, unfinished.

"Go on and say it."

"A black man who... I don't know... You weren't honest with me. You should have told me what you planned to write and let me decide if I wanted to be party to it."

"You're starting with the notion that I knew what it was I was going to write before I got here." Louis looked at her as though he'd explained himself, but when Lydia didn't budge, he said, "Fact is, I don't really have a firm idea of what I'll write. The story could come from... Whatever we find."

"But you know that it'll have to do with race."

"Why would you assume that?"

"There's no assumption about it. I told you. I looked you up. I know what you do."

"A man can't do more than one thing?"

"You can do whatever you like." She shook her head. "Michael was a biologist. He wouldn't have wanted anyone writing something that implied he was anything other than that."

"Like what?"

"An Uncle Tom... some sort of... symbol or... I don't know; that's why I'm asking." Lydia looked at him for a long time and he was silent.

"That's not why I'm here."

"Is there something you want to tell me, Louis?"

"I'm not sure what you mean." With a rattle the heater beneath the window kicked on. The chill air in the room whirled a moment—seeming suddenly colder—before the warm air nudged it aside. The heater was loud enough so that Louis had to raise his voice when he said, "Jane Goodall," hoping to return Lydia to where she'd started.

"Sure." She looked away, nodding. "Sure. Jane Goodall. The epigraph in the Wilton book... At the time that book was published it seemed completely reasonable that the world's preeminent zoologist might argue that Bigfoot could exist. Now?" She shook her head, answering her own question.

"That much has changed?"

Lydia nodded, turning down her mouth. It must have been a regular expression for her; all the wrinkles below her nose seemed to coalesce. That expression must have been why they existed in the first place. "Yes," she said, "Everything has changed. The Pacific Northwest has changed. Places that only five, ten years ago were deep, deep wilderness are now strip malls and housing developments. The entire world has changed."

"...Still a lot of woods out there," Louis said.

"As I said, the whole world has changed since I started doing this: now, everyone's got a high resolution camera in their pocket all the time. In spite of that, instead of seeing more, better quality images of Bigfoot, as one would expect, we're seeing fewer."

"While that might be true," Louis shrugged, "I'd posit, anyone wandering the woods with a cellphone in hand is likely too preoccupied with nailing the perfect selfie to notice the wildlife at all."

Lydia smirked and snorted. "Maybe. I'll tell you what, though, I've spent my career running around the woods, chasing stories, searching out evidence. Back in the heyday, when we found a track, it didn't matter how far outside the paradigm it was, we'd get out the plaster and make a cast. Every discovery seemed like it was leading us toward some certain conclusion. Now, in retrospect, none of it seems to add up to any sum at all." She shrugged. "You get one print that's twenty-two inches long and ten at the width. The next one you get is only sixteen and eight. So, you say, okay, it's a juvenile. Then you get one that's twenty inches long but only seven inches wide and you say, okay, this one's female. But, the thing is, you're not really following evidence. You're making presumptions so that your finds fit into some greater narrative. You find a print with four toes off the front of the foot; you find one with five. You find one that looks like it has an opposable thumb and you say: this must be a different subspecies. In the end, there's a simpler solution: it's fictive. Every bit of it, planted by some conman with too much time on his hands and a need for attention."

With another din of meshing metal parts, the heater wound down. The room was silent.

"What about the Wilton Incident? That's always been considered the benchmark, hasn't it? You were there for that."

The question caught Lydia up for a moment. She looked to the ceiling, her expression clouding. But, then she went on, ignoring it altogether, "We flew down to Texas once, Michael and I. There was a wealthy rancher down there who claimed to have a Bigfoot, encased in ice. Michael and I showed. A lot of people showed: researchers we had connections to, some more amateurish Bigfooters who we always tried to steer clear of, a handful of local media.

"This rancher, he has this 'specimen' in the back of a refrigerated trailer. He lets us go in in small groups to take a peak. Won't let us close enough to touch it and, the thing is, it's dim in there: a single forty watt warm-tone bulb hanging from the ceiling. Michael and I had a look. There was something in there," Lydia closed her eyes and nodded. "This vague, dark mass suspended in the ice. It looked like a man, but enormous. It was very convincing. Well, we all get let out and after everyone's seen it, we get to ask questions, while the news crews stand in the back, taking pictures. Michael asks, 'Why's it so dim in there?' and gets some quick answer about needing to keep the specimen as cold as possible. Well, whatever. Michael and I leave and he says, something to the effect of, 'Well, that was a waste of time.' I start arguing with him—I was really convinced by the thing.

"So, the rancher starts taking it to county fairs and carnivals; taking it around the country. Closest it came to us was Idaho, near the end of the tour, and I convinced Michael we should go and see it once more.

"Well, okay. It's early September and hot. Must have been in the eighties, at least. We get in line, get led into the trailer. There's no A/C running. It must have been ten degrees hotter in there than it was outside. That block of 'ice' is sitting on saw horses at the back of the trailer, not a drop of moisture beneath it. But, you know the sad thing I think about now? That was the most convincing physical evidence I've ever seen. The first time I saw it, in that cold trailer, it looked—it really looked—like there could have been a Bigfoot in there. It really did." She took a breath and exhaled and looked away.

"...Beside the Wilton Incident."

"I'm sorry?"

"The most convincing thing, beside the Wilton Incident."

"Yeah. Of course. We didn't get any physical evidence from that, though... Just the photos and an audio recording—that sort of evidence is easy to dismiss."

"But the bulb tipped Michael off? In the trailer, I mean. That was what made him suspicious?"

She nodded. "And he was right to be, even for how it frustrated me at the time. When you discover a truth, Louis, you don't say, 'handle it gently, don't look at it too closely.' You have confidence that it'll hold. And that anyone will be able to see it for what it is."

"And Marcus Auster isn't showing that kind of confidence."

Looking at Louis from under her brow, Lydia nodded in a slow, deliberate way.

"There's another possibility, too."

She gestured with her can for him to continue.

"That it is real, and that Auster just doesn't have faith in it himself."

She shrugged. "Maybe. That's still nowhere to start, though, is it? You don't know who found it. Or, dressed it. You don't know where it was found. So, fine. Even if it is real, with no way to substantiate it, veracity is moot. If you can't test it, de facto, it is false."

"And you don't want to find out for sure?"

Lydia gave a long, languishing sigh. "That Marcus Auster wouldn't allow photos, samples, that he wouldn't provide the names of the men who brought it to him... That's all the proof I need. I've done this a long time. It's second nature sussing out the bullshit—pardon my French. Auster is full of it. I knew that before he invited me here."

"But you came anyway. There must have been something you thought worthy of looking into."

"Yeah. Okay. Sure. A possibility."

"What if I find it—substantiation that it's real? How will you feel if you passed the opportunity up?"

"There's nothing to find, Louis."

"What if you're wrong?"

She shrugged. "There's still that other issue, even if I thought this thing was worth pursuing... Even if I thought it could be verified."

"Which is?"

"Which is you, Louis."

"Okay," he said. They were silent, watching each other. Louis was the first to blink. He nodded and stood, sidestepping through the narrow space, wavering silently by the door for a moment before saying, "Good night, Lydia," and letting himself out.

The rain was still slashing away, silvery strands of spider's silk glimmering through the darkness.

"Good night, Louis."

THE GRAY MORNING LIGHT leaking through the motel curtains didn't seem as dismal as it had the day before. With only a few hours sleep, Louis felt energized. He'd been up 'til three, compiling a succinct action list that might have looked to anyone else as though he'd jotted it in a matter of minutes, instead of the hours it'd taken.

Coming back to his room, after leaving Lydia, he'd perched himself at the desk with his laptop, trying to assemble a list of directions to take, a list of things to be done.

His being here was grounded on a premise that he was working, and that suddenly felt predicated on Lydia. He needed her. If he gave up the notion that he'd come here to write this story, what little was left?—a mire of depression and self doubt; a mirror, he would have no choice but to examine. The advance would have to be returned. That would be problematic. The money had drifted away over the last few months, like it had been left out in the wind. That was what had brought him to the Peninsula, ostensibly.

—Initially, it was a lie he'd told himself: that his agent might be right, that the quiet of the wilderness was what he needed. That, with quiet, be could finish the book he'd been contracted to write.

The lie hadn't even withstood the drive here: off the highway, in the insulated cabin of the Benz, he'd started hearing the noise of nothing-at-all. Once he noticed that, it occurred to him

how alone he was. On the passenger seat beside him, the manuscript sat like a hitchhiker he regretted having picked up. He
didn't remembered triggering it, but clearly remembered the
burst of damp air that came flooding in when the window slid
down. A moment later, he'd looked in the rearview to see all that
paper swirling above the road. A dizzying wave of relief washed
over him.

That hadn't lasted, either. By the time he checked into the
hotel in Port Angeles, a weight of anxiety had started smothering him. He'd found an office supply store in town and paid to
have the manuscript reprinted from a file on a thumb drive. His
courage had been a self-deceit, and only temporary in whatever
little relief it offered.

After a day of sweating, dread and failing to get anything
meaningful done, he'd stopped trying to delude himself about
why he'd really come to the Peninsula. There was wilderness
everywhere, but he'd chosen this wilderness and that was no
accident. Lydia Swane was here; that was why he had come.
Immediately, he started deceiving himself again; telling himself
he'd landed on an alternative to giving up the money.

Of course, even in Louis's self-deceit, he knew that, objec-
tively, this route and that end were both highly uncertain—
maybe the equivalent of following coin toss determinations at
crossroads and hoping to end up in Graceland, on stage, imitating Elvis. And, although the fantasy of being able to keep the
advance by doing something other than the work he'd been contracted for might have sufficed as an insincere preoccupation, it
seemed almost enough for him to simply latch on to Lydia. As
though, if she were around, he could excuse himself from having to dwell on the reality of why he'd fled here: his recent en-
gagement (which should have been a source of joy but, unac-
countably, wasn't—only another erupting wellspring of
anxiety), his mother, his own past which seemed to be rising like
a wave behind him, swelling up just so it could toss him forward, into an even more tumultuous future.

He tapped the keys, faltered, deleted what he'd done; started again. It was like a game: constructing a tower of verbiage and logic only to reach the inevitable point where it could no longer hold, and the structure collapsed. After deleting all he'd written for the tenth time, he drew back from the keyboard and set his elbows on the table and rested his face in his hands. The exhibit at the museum was to open to the public in two days time. Returning his hands to the keyboard, he entered that as the first item on the list, and then stared at the screen, not knowing how to follow it.

When his cell phone rang, and he saw it was Maria calling, he didn't even consider answering. Switching the ringer off, he tossed the phone away, onto the bed. It landed face down and almost silent, the buzzing dampened by the bedding.

After a moment, he laid his fingers back on the keys and typed out, Keep Lydia engaged.

Looking over what he'd written; the two items seemed like disproportionate characters trying to balance a seesaw: a fat man holding a toddler aloft. Louis highlighted the second item and pasted it back into the document in the top spot. From there, the list seemed to create itself. So...

—He could still write, after all. Even if it was only a few cobbled words, they were cogent.

With his hand on the door handle, preparing to throw himself out into the dim new day, he finally remembered that Maria had called; that he'd intended to text her first thing. Faltering, he got out his phone and, lingering at the door, punched out a quick: Sorry we didn't connect last night. I love you and miss you.

He moved to tuck his phone away but her response appeared immediately: Luv U 2. How's the book coming?

The question sent a charge of anxiety through him; the light of day exposing the errors of a project assembled in darkness. He needed to write a book. All he'd managed was a list. He wrote, Good, guilt spouting up in his stomach to nudge out the anxiety, and sent the text after tacking, Finding my stride, to the end. It managed to dampen the woozy sickness in his gut, if only incrementally.

Slipping the phone into his pocket before her response showed on the screen, (Let's talk tonight. Call me, when you get a chance.) he slipped out the door.

On the blustery balcony, he tried Lydia's room. The curtains in the big window were open, the room beyond, dark. Her bag was leaned against the desk where she'd sat the night before. There was no answer when he knocked.

She was probably at the continental buffet in the lobby, he thought.

Only, she wasn't.

The man at the front desk didn't acknowledge Louis until Louis was well past him, en route to the buffet, when the clerk snapped suddenly, "Room number?"

A flicker of anger ignited in Louis, and he took a deep breath to extinguish it, a flood of air cooling those burgeoning flames. Pulling to a stop, Louis turned. "217."

The man nodded, returning his sullen attention to the desktop where a back page from a newspaper was folded into a tight presentation. Sudoku. A crossword, maybe. Picking up his pencil, the man said nothing.

'Buffet' wasn't the right word to describe the arrangement of food set out in the back corner. The spread was sparse.

The fruit displayed in a suspension of wicker baskets was plastic. A disappointment; an illusion of abundance. A mini fridge held some single serving containers of yogurt, small bottles of OJ and apple juice, diminutive cartons of milk—the kind Louis hadn't seen since grammar school. The carton felt strange in his hand, at once familiar and foreign. It seemed too small. After collecting a bowl and two single serving boxes of bran flakes, Louis sat himself at one of the three round-top tables crammed into the dreary nook at the back of the room. He ate, staring toward the glare of the front window. From here, the day outside looked radiant. Another illusion.

When Louis's cereal was gone, he bussed his table and got a cup of coffee from the carafe. The clerk glared at Louis sidelong, whenever he moved.

When Lydia came in, the desk clerk lifted his chin from his game to give her a halfhearted, "Morning," which she echoed. No room-number request, only the bare pleasantry.

Clearing his throat, Louis offered her his own, "Good morning," the civility of which acted as another cooling deluge, easing his relit anger.

After a quick, rigid smile, Lydia turned to look over the measly bounty.

"Fruit's fake. Everything else is as-presented," Louis said.

She smiled again, but remained mum. With a cup of hot water for tea and her own bowl of cereal, she sat at a table away from his. Once she'd settled in, Louis rose, crossing to her.

"You mind?"

She looked up at him. "Every time I see you, I think it's going to be the last."

"Eventually, you're bound to be right."

She nodded at the chair. "Go ahead."

He sat. "I tried your room earlier."

"So this isn't chance, our meeting again?"

He smiled.

"The exhibit is a fake, Mr. Price. There's no point in anyone pretending otherwise."

"You could be right."

"...You don't see it that way."

He shook his head, scooted his chair closer to the table, leaned in and said, "It doesn't matter how I see it. Our vocations have differing approaches, Lydia..."

She scoffed. "Which do you consider your vocation: talking head or hate monger? Also, what does your 'vocation' have to do with me, or anything here?"

"I'm a writer, Lydia. I wasn't lying when I told you that. That's how I got my start, and I aim to get back at it. Right now, that is the only trade I'm involved in."

"Writers write. So, write. You don't need me for that."

"It's a hell of a story, Lydia. I don't want you to miss out."

"Oh, that's very considerate of you..."

Louis stared at her.

She sighed and leaned away from her food. "Fine. I'll bite. ...Differing goals?"

"Yes, differing goals: your profession requires verification of your suppositions. For me suppositions are only necessary as a starting point. It doesn't matter if I'm wrong in the end."

"Speaking as a writer, or a political analyst?"

Louis smirked, winked coyly "Political analyst is a bit generous."

"Hate monger, then?"

Louis's smile waned. "My mother's white."

"She must be proud. Do honkies feel pride? Are they capable? You're the authority. You tell me."

Putting his smile back on, it looked suddenly fragile, an artifice barely supporting the weight of his cheeks. "I get that you don't agree with what you found online. You should know that was a job for me..."

"So you don't believe the things you said?"

"You're putting words in my mouth."

"So, you do think that white people and black people shouldn't intermingle—that they should live separately, separate neighborhoods, separate schools? You probably should not have sat at my table."

"I never said..."

Lydia leaned aside to fish her phone out of her pocket.

When she started fiddling with the screen, Louis hurried to say, "What I said was that, you know, maybe these neo-nazi's are right. History has sort of proven that white people are incapable of living beside people of color without indiscriminately molesting us. So, maybe colored people should learn our lesson and stay away..."

"And your mother's white. I wonder how you think that makes her feel?"

"It's a political point, not a personal one. My best friend's white, too... Although, he's probably not my friend any more... That isn't relevant. Listen," Louis shrugged, "I've been guilty of hyperbole on occasion. Sometimes you have to exaggerate to make a point. I won't apologize for that. Whiteness gets it own screaming advocates. Why shouldn't color be allowed that same right?"

"I think the world could use less hyperbole in general. Less screaming, specifically."

"Funny thing about hyperbole, it markets a lot easier than nuance..."

"Screaming is never the opposite of screaming, even if it comes from a different direction. It's simply more screaming. The world isn't just a construct of polarities..."

"You can't talk about race until you start talking about race, Lydia..."

"I don't want to talk about race."

"That's fine. I don't, either." Louis looked at her. She said nothing. "I am capable of writing about other things."

"You can write about whatever you like. Don't involve me in it."

He held his hands apart on the table, and stared through the space between them, as though he was holding a magical orb, which would let him see hidden things. "I was thinking about it last night, the best way for us to move forward."

"You," Lydia said, and couldn't help chuckle, "—if you're so determined. Not us. There is no us."

Louis ignored her. "I agree, the museum's a dead end until we can convince Auster to connect us with our hunters—which doesn't seem likely, at least not in the short-term. Obviously, they're the ones we need to get ahold of."

Lydia shook her head. There was no amusement in her tone now. "Again: don't say 'we'. I'm headed back to West Linn today." She stared at Louis for a silent moment. He stared back. "And, to put a point on it, there're almost certainly no 'hunters'."

"I had two trains of thought on that: first, we should go talk to a game warden, see if they know anything which could help. You know, known poachers who work the area, people who've been caught before; places where unusual sightings are common, that sort of thing. Secondly…"

"You are aggravatingly persistent."

"My mother's told me that on occasion, as well."

"So, your plan, pardon my summary, is to cast about aimlessly and hope you land on something of relevance. Is that about the gist of it? A young black man and a honky, old biddy…"

"Enough with the honky stuff, already. I get it."

"It's your word."

"I wouldn't call it 'my word.' You must know how news works in the internet age. It has to be sensational. I understand that you found some stuff online, attributed to me that you find objectionable…"

"It wasn't attributed to you, it was you."

"I understand that. I understand that you're familiar with the kind of work that I've done, interpreting current events and that you don't agree with the conclusions I come to. I understand that. We don't have to agree to be able to work together."

"You have a high way of talking about what you do, for a man who doesn't seem to want to take ownership of it…"

"…What I used to do…" he corrected her, and he said, "I'm writing a book now and there's a different side to what I do and this is it: you and I chasing this thing, my recording the steps we take. That's it for me. That is the story. It doesn't matter to me, in the life of the piece, whether or not we come to a definitive conclusion about the specimen at the museum. What matters is us undertaking the adventure. My recording it. Setting it in prose."

"Okay. Fine. Even if I could forget everything I know about you, that's fine. But, it doesn't matter—if I don't see a way that this will further my research, then it isn't worth my time. Not at all. And, frankly, I do not see this leading anywhere, Louis."

"So what will you do now?"

"Go home. Not waste money and time chasing a fiction."

"So it's money and time. And that's all?"

"Those are two pretty big things, Louis."

"What if I hired you as a guide? Take money out of the equation."

Lydia appraised him silently. "Are you telling me your publisher would finance my coming on?"

Louis nodded. "I believe I can make that happen."

"What are we talking?"

"What are you asking?"

She leaned back and folded her arms over her chest. "Three hundred a day. Plus expenses. And your promise that Michael isn't brought into it. No mention of him in the book. None."

"Agreed. You're on board?" He offered his hand across the table.

Looking away, gnawing on the inside of her cheek, Lydia blew a puff of air out her nose. "What do I have to lose? I'll commit to three days. We can extend it if its seems like this is going anywhere. I'll expect a contract from your publisher by the end of the day."

Nodding, Louis let his hand fall.

THE SKY HAD GIVEN OUT. In Montesano, further from the warming influence of the bay, little shards of ice rained down, stinging like the embers from a sparkler, as Louis and Lydia crossed the parking lot to the Washington Department of Fish and Wildlife. Freezing rain bounced on the pavement and vanished when it stilled, darkening the asphalt, collecting in the grass and making the lawn in front of the building look like stale cupcake frosting. Lydia kept her face held away from the wind, and asked, "So, who's the appointment with?"

"No appointment. We're just gonna see if someone will speak with us," Louis said. He made it a few more paces before noticing Lydia was no longer beside him. Turning, he found her stalled out, staring at him, holding the fringe of her hood against the wind, pellets of ice bouncing from the fabric. "What?"

She shook her head, lowered her face and started forward again, muttering, "Oh, you'll see. I guess we both will."

The chief warden wasn't in, but there was a deputy loitering in a back office who agreed to speak with them.

Louis and Lydia were led into a conference room. The chairs were cheap and the walls had black scuffs, waist high from where the chair-backs had bumped into the drywall, again and again.

After a while, the deputy came in. Introducing himself as Shaw, he sat with a pad of paper to his side, and asked how he could help.

It was obvious Lydia was only along for the ride and so Louis started, asking if he could record, and the deputy didn't have a problem with it, and so Louis pushed his phone toward the center of the table, watching the tracker draw out a few seconds to make sure it was working, and then he said, "I'm Louis Price. This is my consultant, Lydia Swane. We're working on a story about the new exhibit at the Olympic Museum of Crypto-zoological Studies, and we were hoping you could help us out."

Shaw's hand had been wavering near the pad of paper with his pen poised but now he set the pen aside. Pushing the pad away, he straightened up. A droll smirk had grown across his face.

"You've heard about the new exhibit, I take it."

The man nodded, his smirk growing tighter. Addressing Lydia, as though she were sharing in some grand, unspoken joke, he said, "First of its kind, I hear."

"That's what the curator claims," Lydia said.

Louis asked, "Has anyone from the department been out to look at it, yet?"

"I couldn't say. I don't know what they all get up to for leisure."

"I meant officially," Louis said.

The deputy's brow rose. "Officially?"

"Well, you know about what they have out there, yes?"

"I saw a teaser on the channel three news. Sounds like an industrial-grade tourist trap."

"And your department hasn't sent anyone out to take a look?"

The man's smile slipped. He frowned down at the phone, watching the seconds mount up. "Turn that thing off."

Louis held still a moment before leaning forward to pause the recording. Drawing back, he left the phone where it was.

The deputy watched the counter for a moment. When he raised his eyes to Louis, he said, "You're not putting me on record for any of this. Last thing I need is the chief reading about one of his deputies in some parody piece in some lib-tard magazine."

"It's not a magazine. It's for a book I'm working on."

"Irrelevant." The deputy shook his head. "Not happening."

"Will you agree to speak as an undisclosed source?"

The man's laughter was as abrupt as a clap of thunder and dissipated just as quickly. He turned to Lydia with a smile cutting his face wide. "You want me as an unnamed source for a book about a Bigfoot doll in a museum for dopes? That about the measure of it?"

Louis happened a quick look at Lydia. Her face was tense and going red. Louis brought the deputy's attention back. "Everyone likes a good story, especially one on a fun local topic, right? What do you say? Come on, play along."

Shaw gestured—half shrug, half nod. "Yeah. Okay."

Louis nodded to the phone in the center of the table.

Again from the deputy, "Yeah. Okay."

Louis tapped the screen. The recording tracker lurched forward again.

"How 'bout attributing my remarks to Deep Foot? That'd be funny, right?"

"Yeah, sure," Louis said.

Lydia stood suddenly, her chair squawking out from under her.

"Gimme the keys," she said, jabbing an open hand at Louis.

He leaned aside. Plucking the car keys from his pocket, he dumped them into her palm. When he turned back to the deputy, he caught the man tracking Lydia as she went out the door and then, through the wide windows behind Louis's back, as she took off, down the hall. "What's eating her?"

"She hasn't been feeling well."

"She did seem pale," the deputy said.

Rather than dwelling on the statement, Louis hurried on, "So, you were saying no one from the office has been out to look at the exhibit, yet?"

"No," the man said with a chuckle quaking the word. After a moment's thought, the deputy set his hands on the table and leaned toward the phone, saying, "We wouldn't get involved in something like that. There are some hard rules about departmental jurisdiction and we wouldn't want to step on any toes over at the Bureau of Magical Bullshit." The man leaned back to laugh.

Louis gave the deputy a warm, disingenuous smile. He nodded and took a quick note on his own pad of paper (jackass, scrawled illegibly) and said, "That's good. I'll put that in. For the rest of the interview, if you don't mind keeping it straight, I'd appreciate it. Just hard writing this sort of book to begin with, 'cause it's kinda silly. It gets harder when I have to weed through a bunch of stuff that's off tone or off topic. You understand."

The deputy shrugged. "Your call. I feel like I got a lotta good material for this, but if you're not into it..." Another shrug. "Your loss."

"I appreciate it," he said and forced a long silence to try and get some earnestness back into the room. "The director of the museum told us the creature was taken down on the Peninsula. My question for you: What kind of laws might be applicable here? ...Poaching? ...Endangered species regulations? That sort of thing."

"Yeah. Okay. The thing is, all our hunting laws are written to apply to actual breeds of animal, right? Now, I don't know if it's oversight, laziness, or just too much else going on up at the State House, but our legislature seems to have overlooked penning protections for pretend animals. So—no—I'm not really aware of any applicable laws for this kind of thing." He shrugged. "If you happen to see a unicorn on your way home, feel free to bag it. I mean, discharge of firearms is still illegal in public spaces, so you'd have to take that into account. Otherwise, that rainbow-bitch is all yours..."

"Okay." It was getting harder to prop up that warm smile Louis was trying for. "So, no plans to send someone out to look at the specimen at the Museum?"

The deputy's good humor seemed to evaporate in an instant. "Look, this office is not concerned with this sort of thing at all. It would be an enormous waste of our time and limited resources, sending someone out there. No laws have been broken, no one's person or property has been impacted, so far as I know. Now hear: this department is supposed to enforce hunting and fishing laws. More and more often, however, I'll tell ya, we're finding meth labs in cabins. We're nabbing junkies stealing guns to pay for heroin. Excuse me if I find it hard to take this dumb little amusement of yours seriously, but we have a plague of drug issues overrunning this county. It used to be hunters we'd deal with. Half the people we're seeing these days are addicts—and half of them are so far gone, they look like the breathing dead. You have no idea what it's done to this area." Hastily checking his watch, looking so quickly he couldn't possibly have seen the time, the deputy stood and collected his notebook, giving Louis a gesture toward the doorway. The interview was over.

IN THE PASSENGER SEAT, Lydia stared ahead while Louis tossed his bag into the back. After he'd climbed in, pulled the door closed behind himself, and briskly rubbed his hands against the cold, he said, "I hate to say it, but you were right: that was a huge waste of..."

"I can't help you with this, Louis," Lydia announced suddenly, cutting him off. "I'm sorry."

Louis paused, his chest tightening.

"I'm sorry, but I have no desire to get dragged around the Olympic Peninsula so I can be made fun of. I'm done. Take me back to the motel, please."

Louis nodded gently, his head bobbing as though he might faint. Only when he started feeling muzzy did he realize he'd been holding his breath. He gasped and exhaled.

The rain washing down the windshield had made a muddle of everything outside. When Louis hunched forward and pushed the starter, the wipers lunged, plowing through the washout, and the world beyond resolved itself, trees cohering from drab green puddles, the long, gray wad of the Washington Department of Fish and Wildlife returning to rigid form.

On the road, Louis and Lydia were quiet.

The radio muttered, tuned to a public broadcast station. Louis couldn't focus on the chatter; he'd failed at keeping to his action list—hadn't even managed to execute that first item faithfully—keeping Lydia engaged; keeping her contained in this simple story; a story her whole life had been building toward. Even with her still in the seat beside him, it was like she was drawing away, fragmenting into nothingness like a dispersed flock of birds, like paper in the wind. He didn't have the hunters. He didn't have Marcus Auster. Michael Bishop was lost, of course, reassigned to that cosmic agency that doesn't return phone calls. And now Louis had lost Lydia as well; the story wafting away like steam.

And in that dawning absence, Louis's lungs seized up again —a fresh rush of panic overwhelming him, robbing him of his breath. He was suddenly a child again, coerced into the drainage pipe at the end of his grandfather's driveway; ordered to pull out a bung of leaves and decay that had interrupted the flow. Everything came bursting out all at once, from a trickle to a deluge in an instant, dowsing Louis, filling his mouth. Louis was sure he'd drown.

When he'd clambered back out, shaking and gasping into the light of day, Louis opened his eyes to see his grandfather standing over him, laughing. The man turned his pink face away and lurched up the driveway, still laughing. It was a warm day, and eventually Louis's clothes dried, but that feeling of drowning had never really gone away—here it was, rising up once again...

"If we could just find the hunters, Lydia," he half-coughed.

"There aren't any, Louis. Marcus Auster made that thing. Or, had it made. It didn't come from out there." She gazed out the side window at the trees charging past, at the vague grayness slowly consuming everything, oblivious to the way Louis's face had drained, the way his eyelids had started fluttering.

The rain was coming harder, fat wads of sleet slapping the windshield.

The story was dimming away, vanishing. Lydia was going to leave him. And the book... Sixty thousand words already arranged. All he needed was another five thousand to meet his obligation... But, in his head—continuing the rearward rolling momentum of everything else in his life—the cursor was flailing backward, consuming everything it collided with, gobbling up everything he'd created until there would be nothing left: a metaphysical drain in his mind so thirsty that it sucked up everything. There was no escaping it.

The world dimmed away. Louis's head listed to the side.

But then suddenly, Lydia was shouting and the blare of a horn shrieked past and the world outside was a gray smear whipping around them as Lydia grabbed the wheel, yanking the car back into the lane, but overcorrecting.

The sedan bucked and shuddered, catching air for a moment before it flopped gracelessly into the grass at the roadside. A band of evergreen boughs slashed the windshield, smacking and scrapping; Lydia's scream a siren, cutting through it all.

Even when the car had finally settled, the horn continued blaring.

"Take your hand off the horn, Louis," Lydia said, once she'd gotten her voice back.

He was gasping, wide eyed, staring forward.

Unbuckling her seat belt and climbing up in her seat, she knelt sideways to him. Reaching out, she gently tugged his hand from the center of the steering wheel, where it was braced. The shrill bleat of the horn finally died.

Lydia held his hand tight in her own and, with her other hand, stroked his cheek until his attention came around to her.

"You're having another panic attack, Louis. That's all."

She moved her hand to his chest. Even through his thick wool shirt, she could feel his heart clenching anxiously.

"Relax, Louis. Breath," she said. She kept coaching him, speaking softly to him until his breath slowed and he blinked and took his hand back.

LYDIA'S CORRECTION HAD sent the car on a rollercoaster path up a slopping embankment, alongside a stand of cedars. Any closer to the trees and the car might have been totaled... or, worse. Louis got out to survey the situation.

Spatters of mud streaked the hood of the sedan, the fenders and the doors. The wheel wells were bunged up with mud. The axles rested on the ground. It was impossible to tell if there was any damage.

Raising his head, Louis caught Lydia staring at him expectantly through the glass. Her hands were moonlight-white, closed over the crescent of the top of the steering wheel.

He nodded to her, feigning confidence before returning his attention to the bumper, sitting snuggly in the grass. Hunkering down, he got his hands under it and, after yelling, "Ready?" he yelled, "Go!" and lunged forward.

In the same moment, the wheels whirred against the bed of mud. The car heeled back, but wouldn't come free. The moment Louis found he couldn't keep pushing and let go, the car settled back where it had been. The freezing rain was coming faster now, stinging the back of his neck, jittering and clicking off the hood of the car.

He tried once more: "Ready? Go!" lunge. The tires whirred, sending up fountains of mud.

Again, nothing.

Louis straightened, frowning down at the hood of the car. When he heard the airbrakes of a big diesel rig groan and sigh down in the road, he almost forgot the pain in his back—but was reminded when he swung around too sharply. The spasm clenched painfully again. Below, pulled to the shoulder of the road was a massive wrecker, orange lights atop the cab flashing in the dim day.

With care, Louis made his way down the incline to the street.

Letting down the passenger window, when Louis had gotten close, the driver of the tow truck called out, "Little hung up, looks like."

Louis grimaced. "A bit. You think you could help us out?"

The man paused, an expression drawing down his face. "Say, you look familiar. You play for the Seahawks? —No, too small. Help me out—where've I seen that face? You ain't wanted, are you?"

Louis shook his head. "We just need help getting pulled out."

"Sure. Sure. I'll have to charge, though, you understand. I can give you a deal to get it down off that embankment, seeing how my coming along seems serendipitous."

"Okay."

"How's forty bucks sound?"

"That'd be great," Louis said.

"Let me call it in, and I'll meet you up there."

"Great. Great," Louis said and turned and made his way back up the hill.

Lydia had the driver's window down when Louis came back to the car. "You're lucky."

"I know it."

She rolled the window back up without saying anything more.

It took a few tries for the tow driver to get the wrecker backed up at the right angle, with much screeching of the reverse alarm, and when he finally dropped out of the cab, the lean of the truck looked precarious.

Taking a couple twenties from Louis, the guy folded them into his back pocket and set about his work. The bumper was buried so deep in the muck that the tow driver had to dig out narrow holes to get to the tow rings. Laying on his side in the muck, without complaint, he managed to find the rings and set his hooks. He was half covered in mud when he got back on his feet, groaning with every adjustment of his posture.

When he stood up again, he narrowed his eyes on Louis. "It's a fancy car for off-roading. You the hired help?"

"Excuse me?"

"Ain't stolen? I'm just kidding. But really, what do you do for work, to get a car like that?"

"I'm in the entertainment industry."

The man clucked his tongue. "Yup. I guess that's how I know you." The man looked up at the tire marks dug into the embankment above. "I always thought it was Asians supposed to be bad at driving."

"Excuse me?"

The man grinned, showing off his crooked teeth. "That's a joke. You don't have much of a sense of humor, do you?"

"Whatever you say."

"You giving me a bad look? Don't forget, I'm the one helping you out here. I don't have to."

Louis was silent.

The man continued staring at Louis, nodding a silent moment until he turned his attention to the mud-spattered windshield of the car to say, "The woman'll have to get out, before I can hoist the car."

Louis got Lydia out and the pair stood aside while the crane arm on the back of the wrecker dragged the car from the muck with a sucking smack and a roar of engine noise. When the hood was high off the ground, the driver climbed back into the cab and pulled the train slowly down the incline, parking off to the shoulder again, lights still flashing—the orange, a shock of candescence in the dim day.

At the roadside, they all converged, Louis and Lydia standing aside while the truck driver came around the rear of the vehicle.

"Thanks for helping us out," Louis said.

The driver smiled at him and tacked a magnetized, reflective placard on the trunk. It latched on with a hollow thunk. Turning from Louis, he went to the front wheel well where he hunched over and started chaining the tire up to the rig.

Louis came around behind the man and said, "What are you doing?"

"Gotta get her ready for road travel. Reflector and wheel chains are required by law."

"You said you'd get the car off the embankment for forty bucks."

"And I did. It'll be sixty more at the yard, to have the vehicle released."

"You jerking me around? I don't want my car going to the yard. I want you to put it down, so I can get on with my day."

The man was silent, and kept working and wouldn't look at Louis.

"Listen, I don't understand what the issue is here..."

Having finished lashing the tire up, the tow driver glanced over his shoulder at Louis. "I knew I recognized you. See, normally I wouldn't say I have a problem with the blacks, but I'll tell you: I got a problem with you. Awful surprised to see you with a white woman. What is she, your manager? Probably a Jew, I'd guess."

"Let my car down."

"Can't do. Company policy."

Louis looked at the side of the truck. "Yvette's Towing, huh? You wait right here."

Turning from the man, Louis keyed the number on the side of the truck into his phone. The line rang once in his ear, before he heard a phone ringing behind him and he turned back just in time to see the smirking tow truck driver fish his phone from the bib of his overalls.

Louis dumped his phone back into his pocket and walked the slim distance back to the tow driver. "Real funny. Let my car down."

"Told you, can't. Company policy."

"Who's Yvette?"

"My wife."

"How much to let the car down?"

"You asking me to violate company policy?"

"I'm asking you to act like a human being."

"You asking that of a honky?" The man glared at Louis viciously. "See, like I said, I normally don't have issue with the blacks at all. You? You, I don't like."

"What do you want?"

"Hundred dollars."

"This is extortion."

"I'm a business owner and I get to set my own fees—it being a free man's country. Having to deal with someone unsavory as yourself, that comes with an added charge."

Louis's face was getting hot, but he kept his mouth shut and dug a hundred dollars from his wallet. The man took the wad and folded it into his back pocket. Without any hurry, he got the car unchained and unloaded and climbed back up into the cab of the truck.

When Louis turned back to the car, he found Lydia had already taken her spot behind the driver's wheel. Louis went to the window and knocked on the glass. "My car, Lydia. I'm driving."

She shook her head, staring forward rigidly.

"Not kidding, Lydia. My car. I drive."

"Nope," she said flatly—her voice dulled by the glass—and shook her head again.

Louis turned and walked to the passenger door, muttering to himself, "I just can't win today."

He slid into the passenger seat and, when the tow truck pulled away with a big blast from the horn, Louis wound down his window to give the man the finger.

As though choreographed, the truck driver returned the gesture in an instant.

"What was that all about?" Lydia asked.

"Fan of the show," Louis said.

Lydia snorted and was quiet. After a few minutes of driving, the silence between them like a wall, Lydia said, "So, what'd it cost you to get your car back?"

"Hundred and forty."

Lydia whistled. "That and my guide fee—today's turning out to be real pricey, honky-wise, that is."

"Quit it with the honky shit, already."

"That 'honky shit' is your shit, Louis."

"No. No. That honky shit is racist tow truck driver shit."

"Just because he took you for some money, doesn't make him a racist, Louis. Tow drivers and mechanics have been praying on women for millennia, but I wouldn't say that makes them all misogynists."

"I would. But, you're right—taking advantage of me does not make him a racist. His very broad comments about Jews and Asians, I would argue, does."

"I didn't hear him saying anything like that."

"That's fine. Just like every white liberal out there, you don't see racism for two minutes and assume it's been abolished."

"Racism, huh? We can talk about racism, if you want." She cleared her throat. "I was struck by something you said on that internet show, forgive my paraphrasing, ah, something like: 'Whiteness is a disease which might have destroyed this country, if this country could have existed without it.'"

"You don't feel that's a fair assessment?" Louis shrugged. "I can understand that. It probably looks different from a white perspective; that does nothing to change the fact that that's how things are."

"Michael wouldn't have agreed with you, either."

"I think you might be surprised..."

"Okay," she said. She cleared her throat—it resembled a

growl this time—and said, "So, what am I in it?"

"I don't follow, Lydia."

"If being white is inherently evil…"

"I never said inherently evil."

"But that's the implication, isn't it? If whiteness is a disease, then *my* whiteness must have *done* something to my husband."

"I can't answer that. I didn't know him. I don't know anything about your relationship with him."

"I'm asking you what you think. What your supposition is. Do you think he took the path that he did because I held him back? Is that it?"

"No one likes being called out, Lydia. I get that. I get that it makes white people uncomfortable—especially progressives. That's the very point of it."

"So, you'd say—or, I think I imagine you already having come to the conclusion—that Michael's career was hindered by the white people who surrounded him, who loved him."

"I wouldn't say that. I would say it would be foolish to assume he could have succeeded in the way a white man could have, without three times the effort, without five times the luck, and ten times the ability."

"But you didn't answer me. Was I the one holding him back? That's your premise, isn't it? That all whiteness is equal and all of it, equally evil. So, I'm in there too."

"Fine, Lydia. You really wanna go there? Let me tell you about my father. Growing up, my father was my bogeyman. And like any good bogeyman, he was in my home, everyday. He was there whenever I looked in the mirror."

"You're being flippant. It doesn't count if you won't even answer seriously."

Louis ignored her, continuing in the same tedious tone, "When I was a kid, that bogeyman was everywhere—the crack epidemic, gang violence, 'super-predators'… I remember visiting my mother's sister in California and seeing the nightly news and they had this counter running onscreen of homicides, no names, no faces, no bereaved loved ones, just a number that kept ticking upward. That's all black people were or could ever be, a statistic, measuring evil, if not the evil itself. And so, of course whites were right to be afraid. My mother's white and in light of that, she was right to be afraid.

"Her fear was sanctioned. And in my mind, as a kid, my mother and I were just the same—more alike than unalike—and so the bogeyman of blackness seemed just as real, just as terrifying to me as it would have to the snowiest child. The thing is, I didn't know that when our neighbors looked at me they were seeing that bogeyman there, too." He stabbed his finger into his chest, hard enough that it produced a muffled whomp. "When my hand was in my mother's hand, they were watching her escorted by a devil. I had no idea that that was how they saw me. I had no idea until I learned to read their eyes. And once you learn something like that, you're stuck knowing it forever.

"Of course, it was bullshit. My father wasn't a monster. Who knows what he was. I never met the man, but I didn't need to—the world told me who he was and my mother didn't argue it. When I'd ask about him, she'd say he wasn't worth knowing. At first, I'd assumed he was a scoundrel. Then, I began to see my mother's hold on me, her unwillingness to tell me about him, as her way of protecting me from blackness.

"Then, even later, I realized she wasn't even trying to protect me. She was holding me, because she knew I couldn't ever really live in her world. She knew it'd be easier for me in a world she didn't belong to and she couldn't bare the thought of losing me." Louis was quiet a moment. He exhaled. "So that's me, and that's how I can call white people out for their hypocrisy and bullshit: because part of me's still jealous that I should have been able to share in it. At least half of me should have been allowed that. But it was denied to me, of course. Because all the best things, even a simple feeling of superiority, are denied to every person of color, regardless of where they come from. That was the truth I discovered. I wasn't more like my mother than unlike. I was more like some nameless stranger I'd never even met, some murderer on the TV. I wasn't even allowed to fear the thing that I was trained to fear, because I was that very thing. That's the disease of whiteness, Lydia, plainly put. Because its a brain disease like schizophrenia, no matter whiteness's intentions, it is always wrong. It is always misguided."

Lydia was silent, her face a sudden knot.

IN THE NEXT TOWN they came to, Louis convinced Lydia to stop for lunch. She didn't verbally agree (she'd said nearly nothing since Louis's monologue) but she did pull over when a sign advertising "Eats," in neon appeared between the trees.

The diner was dreary inside, the windows cloudy with grease. They were directed to a booth. Lydia ordered hot tea and Louis ordered coffee, and they waited for their food to show, drinking quietly, and avoiding each other's eyes.

Ultimately, Louis couldn't keep up the strained silence, or the sustained evasion and he said, "Can I ask a question?"

"Is it about Michael?"

"Yes."

"You ask a lot of questions that have nothing to do with Bigfoot, for a man purporting to write a book about Bigfoot."

"I'm making conversation. That's what people do."

Lydia went quiet and set her mug down. The cups were mismatched. Hers had a cartoon of two cavemen over a fire, some punchline scrawled beneath. His was a red gingham, almost too effeminate to touch. "Why are you here, Louis? I don't I get it. Auster's a charlatan. If you can't see that at a glance, I can't imagine how you pass yourself off as a writer of any merit."

"I told you. I've read everything you've written." He'd *consumed* it all. Beginning as a child, with *The Wilton Incident: History and Hysteria*, a copy of which he'd found in a box in his mother's closet.

On the face of the book, Michael and Lydia's last names side by side seemed to insist they couldn't be more than colleagues: Bishop and Swane, written in a frail, blue font. The brief bio on the inside page did not mention their marriage. The photo on the backside of the dust jacket had them standing far enough apart so that there was no basis to presume they'd ever stood beside one another before.

He'd read the other books too, over time, borrowed from the library and secreted in his school bag—like they were something of which to be ashamed. At that time, he'd been ashamed of everything. No matter what he did or said, liked or questioned, it seemed to upset someone's idea of what he should be. So, he'd taken to hiding everything.

In adulthood—after his first pay check from the Right World News which wasn't spoken for before it was in-hand—he'd purchased the catalog from an indie bookstore he frequented. The books stayed in a place of prominence on the shelf, side by side and in chronological order, not one of the bindings broken. He knew them too well to warrant rereading. Still, they seemed important to have. Books, he'd known since childhood, were magic. They were keys and they were doorways and were the very lands that those doorways opened to. And, even if you didn't need to go there, sometimes it was crucial just knowing you had the means.

"You're the reason I started writing in the first place," Louis said. "Writing got me into performing. That got me full circle, back to writing."

"So, it's my fault."

"Your books saved my life, Lydia."

"Books don't save lives, Louis, unless you're talking about CPR pamphlets."

"Then you don't know books. Growing up, my mother didn't have much in the way of means or social support. Your books, they set me free. I'd wander the forest around my grandfather's home during the summer, looking for Bigfoot. It kept me sane. It gave me purpose."

It had also kept him out of his grandfather's way, but Louis didn't mention that.

Lydia seemed to weigh his words for a moment. After a breath, she said, "So, you know I've written some books, too. Explain to me how this works—some literary agent sees you on the internet and says to herself, what?—I gotta have that man write me a book about Bigfoot?"

"I wasn't hired to write a book about Bigfoot."

"Yeah. That's what I'm getting at."

"I'm not writing a book *about* Bigfoot. That's what you do."

"Okay..."

"I told you: my process is one of discovery. I'm figuring it out still. Generally, I'm thinking the book will be about you. About your search for Bigfoot."

"There's a problem with that," Lydia said. "I'm not searching for Bigfoot."

"Of course you are, Lydia—you've been searching your whole life."

"And this book of yours, it doesn't have anything to do with race? Nothing at all?"

Louis shook his head. "That's a loaded question, Lydia. When you're a black man, everything has something to do with race. Is the book about race? Yeah, of course it is. 'Cause when it gets published, it won't just be a book, it'll be a book written by a black man, regardless of the content," he said. "No matter what I write about, it'll be about race. My race, at the very least."

"If that's really how you feel, then I don't see how you could possibly write about me, without bringing Michael into it." She straightened, pushing on the lip of the table with her hands. It was bolted to the floor and did not budge. Looking around the restaurant for an anxious moment, she exhaled and leaned forward. "Without bringing who he was into it and who I am and I don't want to be a part of that book. Michael wouldn't have, either."

"You're sure of that?"

"As his widow, I am the authority on what he would have wanted."

Louis said, "I didn't know Michael, but I would suspect that his being black was a bigger part of his identity than he let on to you..."

"He was my husband; don't suggest you know any-one-thing about him that I don't."

"Sure, you were his wife but I..."

"You what?"

"I think I know something about his life you couldn't know."

"Yeah? Which is?"

Louis shrugged. "You see a white girl with a mohawk, you think 'punk.' You see a white guy in a business suit, you think 'business man.' You see a black guy wearing it-doesn't-matter-what-the-fuck, you're thinking 'black man.' He can have a mohawk, he can wear a business suit... or clown suit. It doesn't matter. At the end of the day, the world looks at him and sees a n..."

"Don't say it." There was a sudden, low fire in her voice, and it fell Louis quiet.

She took a sip of tea and swallowed and the expression that flared on her face was like it was sand she'd been made to swallow and she said, "We got pulled over once. In Albuquerque. Michael was driving. The cop came to the window and, before Michael could even ask what was wrong, he was cuffed, and put in the back of the cruiser. I was panicked. I was young. It was alien to me. Michael didn't bat an eye. Well, the cop comes right back to the window and leans in and asks if I'm all right." She let slip an anguished laugh. "Can you imagine? I wanted to scream. I was so angry. Michael had his PhD. I had a Masters of my own. We were in love and in that one moment that cop saw the two of us together and determined that we were something else entirely. Some sort of villainy."

After a moment, Louis said, "It's a common experience for a man of color..."

"I loved Michael. It was my experience, too."

Louis shrugged. "It wasn't you put in that cruiser."

"You're not married, are you?"

"I just got engaged."

"Well, when you're married you'll understand: I *was* in the back of that cruiser, too..."

"That's a sweet notion. Except, you weren't."

The food came.

By the time Louis had finished his meal and placed his balled-up napkin on his plate, Lydia'd taken to staring vacantly at the tines of her fork. She cleared her throat and set the fork aside, plucked the napkin from her lap and laid it over her untouched meal.

LYDIA DIDN'T OFFER Louis the keys when they got outside. She bee-lined to the driver's door, her fists jammed in her pockets, as though defending the honor of the keyring from him.

Even so, on the road, Louis watched the way ahead with the same focused care as if he'd been behind the wheel himself, and when they closed in on a crossroads, he straightened up in his seat, saying, "This left, up here."

"What're you talking about? Evany's straight ahead."

"Left. Left. Take this left," he pointed, his finger jerking, jabbing to the rhythm of his words.

"What're you talking about? That isn't the way, Louis."

"We're not going to Evany."

"The hell we're not."

"Lydia, Lydia, left. Left!" He reached out and set his hand on the wheel and started to push.

"Get your damned hand..." She smacked at his hand but he wouldn't relent.

"You better slow it down, or we're not gonna make that turn."

"We're not going to make that turn!"

"Yeah, we are." He pushed the wheel more insistently, sending the car over the center line.

"Alright! Alright! Let go!"

He let go and she took the turn, but didn't get far down the road before pulling to the shoulder. Killing the engine, she turned to him, glaring.

"Do not touch the wheel, while I'm driving."

"You needed to make that left. You weren't going to make it."

She sighed. "Why did I need to make that left, Louis? We're going back to the motel."

"You agreed to come with me and I have..."

"I told you I was out."

"...We'd already agreed on three hundred a day, Lydia. If you don't want to continue that arrangement, that's fine, but you did agree, and you came out with me. I have things I plan on doing before calling it a day, and just because you want to bail, shouldn't mean that I have to upset my whole schedule. Sorry. You're stuck. I can drive, or you can be my chauffeur, I don't care which—but I can't call it just yet. I still have things I want to get done."

"Things to get done."

"I told you: I had a couple ideas." He ticked off a finger. "Speaking to someone at the Warden's service..."

"That went well."

He ticked a second finger "...There are only about a dozen taxidermists on the Olympic Peninsula that pop up on an online search. I was planning on stopping around, see if we can't find out whose handiwork is at the Museum."

"A phone call couldn't suffice?"

"Phone calls don't make for very good prose."

Lydia looked ahead coldly.

"I'm still planning on getting you your three hundred for the day. You have to be game, though."

"Fine," she said flatly, and started the car. "Don't touch the wheel again."

Louis had picked a route back to Evany that passed near two of the taxidermists on his list. The first was in a derelict strip mall at the gateway of a town that looked near the resolution of its existence—one step from ghost-town status, two long strides from being bulldozed.

Only two of the storefronts were occupied. Every other window, every other door had been curtained with brown paper, brown paper curling away at the edges to expose the dark vacancies beyond. One end of the building hosted a grocer. All the thin traffic in the parking lot seemed headed there. The sole other business, nestled between two empty store fronts, was dark. The sign above the door read, Big Ben's Stuffin' Shop.

Lydia parked out front, keeping the engine running, and Louis kept his mouth shut when she made no move to get out.

Hurrying through the mist to the awning, he found a sign posted in the front door that read, 'By Appt. Call to Schedule.' A phone number was scrawled beneath. Louis thumbed the number into his phone before dashing back to the car.

"Next stop," he announced.

With deliberate care, Lydia pulled back onto the street.

The second shop was an hour away.

The drive was silent between them. It was all Lydia. He'd lost her. Forcing her to tag along for a few hundred dollars hadn't helped a thing. Every mile deeper into the wilderness they traveled, she seemed to pull away from him by some measurable, proportional amount. Eventually, he stopped asking anything of her altogether, and watched out the window at the passing landscape, dark evergreens and the dark mystery of a forest in between.

"THIS CAR WILL NOT make that," Lydia concluded, indicating the washed-out dirt road that snaked off, up an imposing incline. At the roadside, a sign advertising 'Taxidermy' had been nailed to a tree. Lydia slowed the car to a near stop.

Leaning forward and down, his chin almost touching the dash, so that he could see up the length of the driveway—or, what remainder could be seen, there was no end in sight—the dirt tract stretched ahead fifty yards before hitching off behind a rampart of trees. Louis looked to Lydia. "What do you think?"

Apparently, not a lot. She hummed her disapproval in a low monotone.

Aiming his finger at a bed of gravel adjoining the roadside and the base of the driveway, Louis said, "Looks like you can park over there."

Huffing, shaking her head, Lydia parked the car. "How long should I wait before calling the police when you don't return?"

"That's funny. Come on."

"I'm not going up there. That exceeds my responsibilities as chauffeur."

"Chauffeurs only get the paid lunch. The three hundred dollar stipend is reserved for guides. Come on."

The scowl on Lydia's face deepened, but she did get out, closing up her jacket and pulling the hood over her head. They started up the lane. Water ran from everything around them, every branch, every stone, every tangle of moss, limply hanging.

Beyond the first bend in the driveway, the end still couldn't be seen. The wind was loud enough in the boughs so they would have had to shout to be heard. But, neither of them spoke.

Another thirty yards in, the driveway twisted again and, after coming through the long, slow turn, they were rewarded by the end of the trail.

The lot was wide and open, mostly taken up by an uneven gravel dooryard that hosted a menagerie of worn out vehicles, and parts of vehicles. The serrated tops of Douglas Firs surrounded the lot, like some imposing wall meant to dissuade barbarians.

Hanging beside the door of a long shed at the gateway of the parcel, an ornately carved sign read, Taxidermy. It was crookedly carved, but still stood in contrast to the graceless sign at the roadside. That was something hastily deployed after too many calls from customers—this was a work of artistry.

On the other end of the lot was a house which didn't appear as though it was the work of a professional builder. The windows looked scavenged, different styles and sizes—not one of them plumb. The siding was a hash of manufactured materials, wood and metal, clapboard, some patches of roofing shingle and, in one place, a weather worn tarp that bowed and thumped in the wind, collapsing and expanding arrhythmically.

Louis started toward the shed, but stopped some long paces away. The windows were dark. No obvious instruction was posted for what to do outside of business hours. He veered off, heading toward the house. Lydia seemed wary of it—seemed like she wanted to speak up in objection—but in the end, said nothing.

At the door, Louis knocked, backpedaling a pace when it opened.

The man who answered was a giant. Clean shaven, his long hair, black and shiny as the back of a beetle, was slicked away from his forehead. A Hawaiian shirt of gaudy flowers covered his torso, the buttons down the front straining to hold the garment closed. He had the cheekbones of an American Indian, or maybe an Icelander and eyes the color of moonlight on snow. He

looked back and forth between the pair in his dooryard.

"Yes? Did you get your car stuck, coming up the road? I hung that sign for a reason," the man said. His voice was deep and calm and he enunciated every sound with equal emphasis, as though he were reading from a script written in an unfamiliar language.

"We're not stuck," Louis said, "and I didn't see a sign."

"Oh. Okay. Well, I am happy with the religion I already got, so..."

"We're here about taxidermy. You run the shop?"

The man looked back and forth between Louis and Lydia again, his gaze settling on Lydia a little longer than Louis. "Got a squirrel you brought along, or something?"

"We were hoping to talk."

"Oh. Well. Okay. Go on down. I will be after you in a moment."

The man pulled away and shut the door. Louis turned and looked at Lydia. She shrugged and led the way back down to the shed.

They stood under the overhang of the roof and waited.

When the shop owner reemerged from his home, his Hawaiian shirt had been traded for a coarse, blue work shirt. Crossing the lot, he didn't look at either of them. He had to hunch to unlock the door to his shop and, tossing it wide, had to duck to enter.

When the taxidermist struck a switch, the walls lit up, illuminating the trophy heads cluttering the place. Tiny, handwritten price tags dangled from everything, swaying in the disturbed air they'd brought in. The area was narrow and made to seem even tighter by the counter running through it. Crossing to the far side, the taxidermist said, "What kind of animal you got?"

Behind him, a doorway was curtained off. His workshop must have hidden behind it.

"Well..." Louis started.

The man craned around to look at the wall behind him. "You after something pre-finished, then? This is most of what I have on hand right now."

Louis brought the man's attention back when he said, "Actually, we were interested in a piece that's elsewhere."

The man turned to Louis. "What, like consignment? I do not understand." Looking to Lydia again, the man seemed suddenly hypnotized.

"We're here looking into..." Louis's words were cut short when the man snapped his fingers abruptly.

Shaking a finger at Lydia, the giant said, "Lydia Swane, isn't it? That's why I recognize you."

Lydia was caught off guard.

"I saw you speak at a conference in Portland some years back. On the Trail of Bigfoot, I believe was what your presentation was called." His voice modulated into something that might have been excitement, or maybe he had just stood a little straighter. "Oh. Well. I got something to show you."

Lydia didn't get a word out. The man had already turned, bulldozing through the curtain behind him. A moment later, the giant bustled back through the curtain, getting tangled up a moment. Wresting his way free, he took care to protect a paper-wrapped parcel cradled in his hands. "Name's Clyde Whitethunder, by the way. Sorry—I do not think I introduced myself."

Lydia opened her mouth to dismiss the apology, but Clyde was already distracted again, setting down his parcel and pulling the paper apart. When he was done, and the article was naked, and he'd set it out on the counter, Louis wasn't quite sure what had been uncovered. He leaned close and Lydia came up beside him, leaning as well.

"Go ahead. You can pick it up."

Lydia reached forward and gently took it in both hands.

In the flowing shadows, Louis could see that it was a plaster cast of a foot. In Clyde's enormous hands it had seemed unremarkable, but in Lydia's grasp it was clearly humungous.

Humming a note, Lydia turned the cast in the light, blue light spilling into the shallows as she moved it. "Normally you'd see a much broader heel and not nearly this much arch to the sole." She looked up at him and, setting the impression down, said, "I'd guess it's human. A very large human, by the looks."

Clyde didn't seem disappointed. He nodded vehemently. "That is what I thought, too. Thing is, I found it out in my back-yard maybe a half mile from my house. In some snow. That really cold winter a couple years ago. I do not know what kind of giant, crazy man walks around barefoot in the snow. There is nothing back there. Nothing at all."

This clearly piqued Lydia's attention. "You follow the trail?"

"Tried. Lost it in a boulder field a mile or so out. Thing is, nothing out there, either. Not in that direction. It's all government land." He nodded at the cast in Lydia's hands. "By my measuring, that's a size sixteen shoe. That is a very big shoe."

"Not unheard of," Lydia muttered, staring at the thing.

"No, but that is a big man to be walking around in the woods barefoot in the snow, miles from anything."

"Indeed it is," Lydia said and moved to hand the thing back to Clyde.

He didn't reach for it. "Would you like it? The price is negotiable."

"My collection's pretty filled out right now, but thanks." She thrust the cast again. Still, he didn't take it.

"I am not lying to you."

"I didn't say you were. I just... My collection's very full. I'm not really adding much to it, these days."

"I got some pictures up at the house of the trail I followed. Would you like to see them?"

Louis could tell Lydia was getting uncomfortable so he cut into the exchange, "Actually, Clyde, we came here to ask you some questions that are right on topic."

Clyde turned to Louis. "That so? Well. Okay. Ask."

"I suppose you heard about the new exhibit opening up, down at the Olympic Museum..."

"Yes. I have heard of that."

"Seen it?"

The man screwed up his face. "I understood it was not opening until Saturday. I do not need to see it, in any case. That man down there is a conman. I tried bringing my cast to him and he asked how many more I could make. Wanted to sell them as souvenirs, is my belief. I took the cast back. I will not do business with a man like that." He nodded at the cast in Lydia's hands, and made a move to collect it from her while saying, "That is why I am still holding onto it. It is for sale to the right person, though."

"On second thought," she said, holding the thing a little closer, "maybe I will take a look at those photos."

The walls shook when he knocked the counter with his thigh. Hurrying outside, he said, "Right back. Yup. I will be right back."

Louis caught sight of Clyde, through the window at the front of the shed, scrambling across the driveway, up the little incline to his house.

WHEN CLYDE RETURNED, he had a fat manilla envelope in one hand, a stack of paperbacks tucked in his opposite arm. He set the books aside. They were all familiar to Louis: books he'd read as a boy, books that were assembled on a shelf in his home. They were familiar to Lydia, as well: she'd had a hand in writing them.

Unwinding the string tie from the red cardboard button at the mouth of the envelope, Clyde dumped the contents onto the countertop. A stash of photographs, little baggies, mini cassettes and loose leaves of paper came spilling out.

Lydia took a step forward as Clyde laid his palm on the pile and spread the mess a little wider.

"Is all this..." Lydia started.

Without taking his attention from his task, Clyde made a little motion with his head over his shoulder, indicating the direction of the woods behind his shack, behind his home. "It is all from my backyard. I have seen a great many things back there... Here they are," he announced, pulling a trio of five by seven prints from the mess. Louis caught a glance at them as Clyde handed them over to Lydia. They looked like they might be duplicates. They were all in the same color palette: white and gray —a bruise tinge in the cloudy sky, the only hint of color.

Lydia stared for a moment at the first in the stack of photos before handing it along to Louis. It was a winter scene. Trees doused in snow. He had to hold the photo close to his face to see the real subject—dents in the cladding of snow, a winding route of prints leading through the trees.

Lydia lifted her head and asked, "You said all of this is from your backyard?"

"Oh, well. Yes. I mean, when I say 'my backyard' you have to understand, I am talking... Well, my land goes back about twenty acres and there is government land beyond that that I consider my backyard as well. But, yes, I only travel on foot for my research."

"The mini cassettes?"

"Calls. You know, mating calls. They are all from back there, as well. I do not use the mini cassettes anymore, though. I have moved over to digital. There are more photos and recordings on the computer, much more than can be kept in an envelope..."

Lydia had passed the other photos over to Louis, and he gave them a cursory inspection before returning his attention to Lydia. She'd come closer to the counter and had started pawing at the items piled there with a gentle, curious finger. "And the baggies?"

"Samples, and I have a tooth, that I cannot identify." He pushed a bag from the pile, a little closer to Lydia. Inside was a tooth.

"Do you mind?"

"Oh. Well. I would not have brought them down if I did not think you would like to see them."

Lydia picked a small sample bag from the assortment. There was a bouquet of short hairs inside. "Sure you don't mind?"

"Are you joking? Your coming here is... No. Please. Have at it."

She smiled and dug into her pocket, pulling out a slim leather folio that was held closed with a length of rawhide strapping. Setting it on the counter, she untied the strip and opened the bifold, exposing a small assortment of delicate tools. With a pair of tweezers, she snagged a single strand of fur from Clyde's baggie and then took a slim magnifying glass from the satchel and leaned in close to examine the specimen. She only looked for a few moments, before putting the magnifying glass down, tucking the sample back into the bag and sealing it up again.

"Bear, right?" Clyde said, nodding shallowly.

Lydia nodded, too.

"That is what I thought." He shrugged. "It is hard, though. Discoveries are so seldom, whenever you get anything there is just so much excitement. Even after you get to really look at it and think that it is not really what you were after, it is still hard to let go of. Oh, well."

She nodded again. "You said everything came from back there, behind your house?"

"Yes. That is correct," Clyde nodded, and when Lydia set the little baggie near the pile, Clyde reached out and snatched it up and set it further away from the rest of the things as though it might be some sort of contagion, spreading rash, mundane reality on everything else.

"You mind showing me where that trail led?"

Clyde didn't mind. He nodded eagerly, before turning to Louis. "You think you can make it, fella? Have you got good shoes?" The taxidermist leaned over the counter to look at Louis's feet. Satisfied with the look of Louis's boots, the giant returned his attention to Lydia. "Well. It is getting late in the day. If we are going to go, we had better do it now."

He made her sign all his books before they left the shop.

BENEATH THE FOREST canopy, it was impossible to tell if it was still raining in the world above the trees. Water sloughed from every surface: the quivering leaves, the long, lacy shawls of moss. Out of season, the ferns on the forest floor were yellowed and brown, laying flat, returning to the soil. Dampness darkened the smooth tops of stones.

Clyde led them up a steep hill, stabbing the land before him with the foot of a walking stick, following an ill-defined path. Turning the curve of the hill, they passed an opening in the canopy where, at a different time of year there might have been a view. Not today. Today, all that could be seen was a broad, impenetrable pillow of cloud. In the open, it was apparent the rain had ceased, but that sky made no subtle indication that it would begin again, and soon. They continued on, crossing the rounded face of the hill, back into the cover of the forest. A short distance in, Clyde stopped, waiting for the other two to catch up. Or, more specifically, waiting for Lydia. He seemed to have no use for Louis at all. He seemed to have forgotten that Louis was even there. Pointing out toward the undulation of the valley, for Lydia to see, Clyde said, "That is where I first noticed the tracks."

He traced his finger along the bowl of the valley, drawing his finger down to a basin below where a rivulet was feeding from the runoff around it and syphoning the pooling water into a trough that passed below them and sprayed off the edge of a cliff, the height of which was impossible to judge from where they stood. It must have been high: when the wind rose, the water frothed in the air.

Lydia asked, "What brought you out here?"

"The same thing that compelled me to buy this land. I am a Bigfooter, even if only an amateur. All I have ever wanted is to see one for myself. I do not care if I can prove it to others. I know that they are out here. One of these days, I am going to meet one."

"It looks pretty steep." Lydia redirected the conversation back to the bowl of the valley below.

"It is steeper than it looks. I would not go down into it. That was something else that drew my attention. I had to go..." Again, the man pointed out a route, tracing it through the air. "...along the ridge there and catch up with it on the other side."

"Strange that whatever left those tracks wouldn't have taken the same route."

"I thought the very same. I figured, on account of all the moisture working its way down to the basin there, that there was some foliage she was after."

"Any indication down below that that's what it was?"

Clyde shook his head. "I am afraid not. Just the tracks."

Louis had finally caught up, but even now he hung back, listening. An outsider. An invisible observer. Nothing more.

"The hillsides were all covered in snow. Down there it was muddy. I looked with my binoculars. There was not any vegetation that I could see. Maybe I was wrong. I did not want to try to get down there. I was afraid I would not be able to get back up." Clyde finally turned from the landscape to look at her.

"She could have been after insects."

"And we're calling it a 'she' because of the narrowness of the foot?" Louis asked, to prove he knew the answer. No one seemed impressed.

Lydia nodded and said to the wilderness ahead, "That characteristic tends to be attributed to females..."

Clyde let loose a chuckle, drawing Lydia's scrutiny. "I am sorry. I was just remembering the talk you gave in Portland. About the pitfalls of making assumptions. Those were some unhappy men in that crowd. Particularly Tom... what was his name? The man who spoke before you."

"Caron."

"That is right. Tom Caron was his name." The man laughed out toward the trees, the sound booming. A moment later, a gust of wind set free a shaker of rain, ticking across the ground away from their feet. Clyde looked at Lydia. "Do you want to keep going? The boulder field where I lost the trail is up a little further."

Lydia looked across the sky. "You think the rain'll hold off?"

"No," Clyde said, "But we might not get caught in it, just going a little further."

"Alright, then." Lydia nodded and Clyde struck out again, leading the charge with a definitive stab of his walking stick.

They rounded the lip of the valley, Louis at the back of the pack once more, pausing now and then to peer into the forest below. He wished he had a photographer with him. The view from up here—trees clinging to the impossibly vertical hillside, everything half eaten in gray—was striking. Maybe he'd try talking his agent, Vivian, into sending one. The idea didn't seem as implausible as it should have. Louis realized he was deluding himself, and quickly dropped the thought altogether.

At the opposite bank of the valley, the rain began again, pattering lightly on the trees above and making everything on the forest floor jitter. Through the boughs ahead, Louis could just start to make out the boulder field Clyde had described when, coming down the incline toward it, Clyde suddenly froze, drawing up his hand to still the others.

They all stopped, leaning forward to listen. Other than the increasing fidgeting of the rain, Louis couldn't hear anything at all. Still, they remained frozen, Clyde's hand held aloft.

After a few more moments, Lydia shifted carefully forward, closing in on Clyde. Louis followed suit, landing at Clyde's other elbow a moment after Lydia.

"What is it?" Lydia whispered, staring forward into the gray, ambiguous panorama below them—a jumble of black tree-spires and amorphous blights of fog.

"Did you not hear it?"

Lydia shook her head and leaned in more intently.

"What was it?" Louis asked in Clyde' opposite ear.

"Sounded like a call to me. There! There!" he whispered urgently and raised a finger to his ear, as though maybe that was where the sound had originated. "Did you hear that?"

Louis hadn't heard a thing.

Then, the forest came suddenly alive: rain dumping down, full force. The view grayed off to nothingness in an instant. The rush of rain nixing the sound of anything else, Clyde let his hand fall. Shrugging, almost shouting to overcome the clamor filling the forest, he said, "I suppose that is a sign. We should head back."

They turned.

Louis was happy they hadn't gone any further down the incline. As it was, the long grass laying flat on the hillside was slick and hard to navigate.

Pulling the hood of his rain jacket over his head, Louis marched forward with his gaze aimed at the ground. A gust of wind rose and knocked the hood off and when he went to set it right again, it had filled with water. He was doused, water rushing under his jacket, soaking his shirt front and back. The sudden cold made his whole body clench.

IN CLYDE'S DRIVEWAY, the giant insisted Louis and Lydia come inside to warm themselves and dry their clothes. Louis was shaking too hard to argue.

The place was not as ramshackle inside as it seemed from out. The living room was cozy and warm and smelled like a barn—the sweetness of dry hay and the must of animal dander, though there was no other sign of an animal in the house. The man gave Louis a heavy bathrobe to wear—it was ridiculous; so large it made Louis feel like a child. The sleeves covered his hands and were too wide to stay in place when he rolled them up.

Lydia got a pair of old fashioned pajamas. In the getup, she looked like a proper old lady, someone in whose hands a knitting needle would seem perfectly placed.

Returning to the room, after having loaded their clothes into the dryer, Clyde crossed to the wood stove in the corner to load in a log.

There, he muttered, "I am so sorry about Michael," so quietly into the mouth of the stove that Louis thought Lydia must not have heard. She did not respond.

Shutting the door to the stove, Clyde returned to his armchair, where a steaming cup of tea waited on an end table just beside.

Lydia fussed with the pajamas. "I'm lucky you had these on hand."

Clyde nodded. "They belonged to my wife. I suppose they belong now to my ex-wife. She has made no attempt to collect them. I have had no good reason for having kept them. But now, they have found their use. Sometimes, you must trust that things will have their place."

Louis said, "You've found a lot of signs of Bigfoot. Are they all from back there, in the area you showed us?"

"It has occurred to me that the area behind my house could be part of a migratory route."

Lydia and Louis were quiet, waiting for Clyde to continue.

After a moment, staring toward the flickering orange window in the stove, he did. "I have found that calls tend to increase in frequency starting in the late fall and lasting until early spring. In the summertime, I have never heard the call."

Lydia nodded. "So, perhaps, it's a wintering area? That would make sense for the colder months for them to come down out of the higher elevations."

"That is the same conclusion I have come to."

Louis stood up. Outside, the day had vanished, and he'd intended to call Maria. "Do you mind if I..."

Clyde nodded toward the hallway at the back of the living room. "Please, treat my home as if it were your own."

Louis nodded and went down the hall.

The bathroom was hot with the dryer running. Lint dust drifted about like dry snow. He closed the door behind him and closed the lid to the toilet and sat down. Pulling his phone from his pocket, when he swiped his finger across the screen, all he got was the red indicator that the battery was shot. It faded away in an instant.

Standing, he floundered a moment.

Opening the vanity, he found nothing interesting inside—a tube of toothpaste, some antibacterial ointment that had gone past its 'good by' date, a bottle of aspirin and an opened four pack of bar soap, stood on end, the plastic-wrap packaging in tatters. In a cupboard beside the tub, he found a box of men's hair dye. Black.

Louis frowned.

Shutting the cupboard, he went out into the hall, pausing when something at the edge of a darkened doorway caught his attention. From the living room, the sound of Lydia's and Clyde's voices drifted down to him. The doorway was lit. Neither of them were in sight.

Reaching into the darkness of the room, Louis felt around on the wall, until his hand brushed the light switch. A muted light spilled from a ceiling fixture, the color of a stained coffee filter, specks of insect carcasses littering the topside of the glass.

Boxes and framed pictures and mounds of clothing were piled in the center of the room. A path had been maintained around the perimeter, but other than that, there was no room for anything else inside. He looked down. Beside the door was a short row of shoes and boots, every one of them enormous. Placing his own foot beside the work boot closest to him, his own boot seemed minuscule. Crouching, he pulled the tongue down to look at the faded label sewn inside. It was size sixteen. Louis rose back up and turned off the light.

Back in the living room, he couldn't help his attention falling to Clyde's feet.

They were enormous, and Louis couldn't help imagining the man stepping into a cold frame of snow, leaving a perfect print to fill with plaster. Clyde was saying, "And the Klallam have tales of another tribe occupying these lands. A tribe of giants. I believe these are the Bigfoot people speak of today and it is my belief that I am a descendant of that tribe."

Lydia was quiet while Louis crossed the room, back to his seat, taking up his own cup of tea. It was finally cool enough to hold without searing his hand.

"It is a shocking assertion, I know. But I believe it to be true. I feel I have a connection to the land that cannot otherwise be explained. I also believe that it may be part of the reason that the Bigfoot have chosen this as their wintering ground. I believe that they can sense I am one of them in the same way I sense it, and that they long for contact in the same way I do."

Lydia was quiet, still.

"You may think it foolish, what I believe."

She shook her head and seemed to examine him more closely for a moment. Louis couldn't tell if she was searching for signs of insanity, or some illusive, bestial attribute. She said, "Have you ever considered taking a DNA test?"

The man shook his head. "I have not."

"Well, they've come a long way in recent years. There are ones available now which can identify your entire lineage."

"And what would that prove?"

Lydia frowned. "Well, it could prove your suspicions."

"The kinship I feel is not a matter of genetics. It is here," he said and thumped his hand on his chest. "It is when I breath." He took a deep breath and exhaled. "What is outside of me, I recognize as my own. That is what brought me to this place: it is my home. It was my home before I ever saw it. I could taste it in the air. It was a spice which already existed inside me. It is the salt of which I am made."

THE ENCOUNTER WITH Clyde had obviously turned Lydia's mood; the radiance from the dash lights illuminated a slight, contented smile creasing her face. Bowed toward the wheel, she drove slowly. Beyond the short, spangled boundary of the headlights flaring against a steady rain, everything was abysmal blindness.

"An interesting guy," she said, after a few moments of silence.

"Clyde?"

"I take it he didn't have the same affect on you."

"You think he's credible?"

She shrugged, a tiny gesture, and was quiet a moment before she said, "There's never been any fossil, or other physical evidence that could rule it out."

"Maybe that's our starting point."

Lydia made a noise in her throat, a quick, dismissive grunt.

After a moment, Louis said, "I wrote a column for the *Seattle Independent Sentinel,* before my gig on the *Right World News.* It started out as kind of a spoof based on *The Modern Bigfooter's Guide to Field Research.* I really liked that book when I was a kid. I'd use the same methodology but apply it in ways it wasn't meant to be. So, the premise was that, instead of searching for Bigfoot, or whatever, I was searching for signs of an elusive American Dream in depressed urban areas. It was all written in this tongue-in-cheek kind of way."

Lydia smirked reluctantly. "I like that. Clever. Searching for something that might not actually exist."

"I don't know. Everyone seemed to expect me to write about race, and I guess it was my way of meeting that expectation without getting swallowed up in it." He shrugged. "I guess Charlie Puelle stumbled on it and he really liked it—the outrageousness, the tone."

"This is…"

"Right… He asked me to come on the show, play this character I'd sort of invented in the column."

"And you agreed?"

"Don't feign shock. You already know I did. It was money, Lydia. Real money. The *Sentinel* was paying me a hundred dollars per column. That's nowhere near a minimum wage income. This was making me actual money. Career money."

"He's a fucking fascist, Louis."

"He's an entrepreneur; an opportunist, if anything… We became friends. He was white, I was black but in a lot of ways, how we grew up was kind of parallel. I grew up in a white environment, where I was an outcast. He'd grown up in a black neighborhood and was always getting beat up and… I don't know, it was just easy to identify with the stories he'd tell me, even though I had no frame of reference for them.

"Anyhow, he started having me on more and more frequently and I started making more and more money for my appearances—his audience, it seemed was really hungry for a heel, a villain…"

"I know what a heel is."

"Well, the character just became more and more extreme. More hyperbolic. More of a character."

"So, it was all an act? Charlie, what's his face, Mr. Right World News himself, is that it for him, too?"

"It's a business. He's making a product. —I think that's always been his position."

"A product that misinforms and incites rage," Lydia said and sighed violently.

Louis shrugged, the gesture lost in the darkness. "People can be dumb and ill-informed if they want. That's their right.

You know, there are two people culpable for a lie, the person who tells it and the person who believes it."

"Wow. That's awful, Louis."

"Is it awful? I guess. It also isn't my problem…"

"It's everyone's problem Louis… Is that what… Is that why you've been having these panic attacks?" Lydia stole a glance at him, silently. He was quiet. She nodded after a moment. "And you think this story might be a bridge for you into something else."

"I always liked your books, Lydia. In a lot of ways, they got me here, made me into the person I am."

Lydia was silent.

"'When you find a track, follow it as far as it can take you,' that's what you said in the postscript to the *Modern Bigfooter's Guide*. I've always followed that advice."

"You know what I think? I think if you want to write something else, you should do it. I just don't want you writing about me."

He looked at Lydia, the blue from the dash lights bathing her features. "I really need you now, Lydia. I really need you."

"I'm sorry, Louis. You can't need me. We don't even know each other."

They were both silent for a long moment.

Lydia sighed. "Besides," she said, "there's still no starting point. This is just a bunch of dead ends, this whole business."

"What about Clyde?"

"What about him?"

"The museum's opening the exhibit tomorrow…"

"And?"

"Well, you think Clyde might be credible. Maybe, seeing the exhibit, he could get a feeling of whether or not it's legit." In the glow of the dash light, Lydia's smile had vanished. She stared forward intently. "This is our track, Lydia. I think we need to follow it."

She didn't say no. Tapping her fingers against the steering wheel, she seemed to be struggling to find the word.

THE LINE FOR THE Olympic Museum of Cryptozoological Studies ran out the front door. It curled down the sidewalk along the face of the building and snaked off around the corner to the parking lot, already so full that the incoming traffic had warranted a detail from the Evany PD: two uniformed cops at the mouth of the entrance, turning cars away.

Parking on the roadside had filled hours ago, and so people were informed that, if they had any desire to see the museum's newest exhibit, they would have to park in upper Evany and walk the mile back down. Some hearty souls had taken the instruction—intermittent bands of tourists trundled down the hill to join the end of the queue.

Louis and Lydia and the hulking mass of Clyde Whitethunder had shown early. Even so, they should have come sooner. Arriving in the stubborn final throws of a January nighttime, they'd still been greeted by a line some two hundred visitors long. Those nearest the entrance were swaddled in sleeping bags. The atmosphere was jubilant: the greatest zoological find of the millennia was only a few hours away from its first public exposition—or, it might be the greatest fraud of the new age. No one seemed to care, particularly, which they would find inside.

Slowly, the day had graduated from a black where streetlights spangled to a muted gray where nothing glimmered at all.

A team of museum employees worked the line, hocking t-shirts and cheap, yellow ponchos and cups of coffee and mulled cider, steaming in the day, but barely lukewarm in the hand.

They'd waited in the cold a long time, Louis shuffling to keep warm, yawning to keep awake. For him, it had been a long day before the sun even rose, and last night had lasted well past when it should've. Rain slowing the drive, by the time he'd gotten into his room, it felt too late to call Maria.

He had two voice mails, one from her and one from Vivian. He called Vivian back—the message had sounded urgent. When she picked up, her voice was thick with sleep, (East Coast time) but she insisted it wasn't too late, "No," she said, "it's important we talk." Stifling a yawn, she said, "What's this about a guide?"

"Right," Louis paced, watching his feet. "Her name's Lydia Swane. It's three hundred a day and..."

"I got the message, Louis. What I'm asking is, why in the world do you need a guide?"

"Right. So, I was blocked, right?"

"I remember," she said.

"Just hear me out. You suggested I get out of the city, right? Clear my head? So, I'm out here on the Peninsula, and there's this tourist museum—claiming to have, get this, the first ever Sasquatch specimen..."

The silence on the other end of the line stopped him talking.

A moment later, Vivian's sigh bellowed in his ear. "Louis. You've been given three extensions. You only have five thousand words left to meet the obligations of your contract. Finish the work, Louis. Houghton and Hall is expecting final pages. I won't say it again: finish the work."

Silence. She'd hung up.

He climbed into bed.

Unable to sleep, he clambered back out an hour later to saddle up to his computer. The chair was cold, with only his briefs as a buffer.

For lack of any magic verbiage to turn Vivian around, he decided to look into the business of Clyde Whitethunder. It was a short investigation. In a matter of web pages, Louis learned that the cobbled home bordering the Olympic National Forrest was owned by a man named Fredric Haake. A few more pages got him to a photo of that man—a blonde giant who'd been a power player in North Pacific real estate some fifteen years prior. He found an article from 2001 about a hunting accident. After that, the man seemed to have vanished. The best photo of him—standing amongst a crew of colleagues—wasn't great, but enlarged it was easy enough to see that he and Clyde Whitethunder not only shared the same giant physique but also the same face.

Louis shut down the computer.

Back in bed, he stared into the imperfect darkness above him—the blinds in the window thrown across the ceiling in a silvery negative. Whitethunder was a fraud, a character. Minus the promised three hundred dollars a day, he was also the only thing keeping Lydia around.

Rising again after only a few restless hours, Louis left his room to find the parking lot enveloping the motel had filled. It was still early enough so that there was no competition for seats in the breakfast nook. Passing the morning clerk, Louis was greeted with a cold, "Room number?"

"217," Louis muttered without turning. His stomach was uneasy.

Lydia came in awhile later—through the window at the front of the lobby, the world was still mired in nighttime.

"Morning, ma'm," from the clerk.

A light, "Morning," from her. She delivered a "Morning," to Louis, as well.

Louis blinked and nodded, too tired to speak, too sleep-numb to harbor any anger at all.

Sitting across from him with a bowl of yogurt and a bottle of orange juice, Lydia frowned at his cup of coffee and said, "That's not much of a breakfast."

Louis didn't answer. Pulling a folded check from his pocket, he set it on the table. Spreading it wide, he nudged it toward her.

Lydia gave the slip a frown.

"My agent thought it best not to have a contract."

"That's a personal check, Louis." She wouldn't touch it.

"It's fine. It's easier this way, as far as accounting goes."

She stayed as she was; her hands where they were.

"Go ahead. Don't worry. I'll get reimbursed." He nudged it an inch further.

She pushed it back his way. "Keep it, Louis. I'm not taking your money."

He didn't move.

She gave the check another prod. "I'm on board. I think you were right, Louis. I think there may be something here. I think Clyde's going to led us right to it."

There was something wrong with the coffee in Louis's cup. His stomach twisted.

IT WAS NEARING NOON when the threesome made it through the doors of the museum. Any satisfaction at that progress was instantly frustrated by the fact that they were still in line; the ticket kiosk still twenty paces off. There, the line broke apart, only to recommence at the entrance to the exhibit space. The place was filled with echoing chatter; the clap of shoes, laughter.

Louis's stomach tightened. He really should have eaten something for breakfast. Now, he was starting to feel lightheaded. Drawing himself up on his tip toes, he scanned the snaking line beyond the stanchion. It wound into the museum, past exhibits in which no one seemed to have any interest. He dropped back to his heels.

"I'm gonna see if the gift shop has any food. Anyone want anything?"

Lydia shook her head.

Clyde Whitethunder said, "The entrance fee alone is far more money than I believe this enterprise deserves."

Louis skirted out of the queue and, dodging through a mass of lingering patrons in the center of the lobby, ducked under the rope and stanchion and hopped into line for the gift shop. It advanced no more quickly than the ticket line, but Louis spotted a cooler in the corner full of soda-pop, an arrangement of junk food displayed on the shelves beside it. After getting through the door, Louis grabbed a bottle of cola and a couple meal bars and slipped back in line.

Behind the counter, at the cashier's side, Marcus Auster's expression sank when he caught sight of Louis. In an instant, the man reapplied his smile to offer a few words to a customer, and resumed his duties: carefully watching every move of the girl at the register and keeping an eye on the flow of people through the shop.

When it was Louis's turn, Auster stepped forward and said, "Come to have another look, have you?—Mr. Price, wasn't it?"

"That's right." Louis looked around. "Good turnout. You must be pleased."

"Say," Auster said, narrowing his eyes to look past Louis's shoulder, "That isn't Clyde Whitethunder back there, is it?"

Louis turned back. A head taller than anyone else in the place, Clyde was impossible to overlook. Facing Auster again, Louis shook his head decisively and said, "No. That man's name is Fredric Haake."

Marcus frowned, unconvinced. "Well, I should hope it's not Clyde Whitethunder. He's been banned from this establishment."

Louis paid and, collecting his things, gave Auster a, "Congratulations, by the way."

Marcus gave a terse nod back, and Louis moved away.

Before he'd even made it out of the door of the gift shop, his attention was piqued by a sudden commotion in the lobby. A clap of shoes echoed from the walls. People shuffled. A tide of gasps surged. And then, cutting through it all, a low grumbling like the noise of a cow—a single man's indistinguishable voice warbling up in a tumult.

Clyde.

Louis paused a moment, closing his eyes and cursing himself. But when the commotion only grew, he started forward again, a single, bitter utterance falling from his mouth, "Shit."

Hurrying now, clipping a man with his shoulder, Louis's bottle of cola slipped from his hand. It hit the ground, hissing and spraying. A woman squealed, scampering away.

The man grumbled. Louis apologized and turned, catching sight of the frothing bottle rolling away in an arc, inciting a panic in the crowd before disappearing into a wilderness of legs. He didn't go after it. His attention was brought back around by Clyde's voice bellowing, "It is my right to see my ancestor!"

Whatever the clerk's response was lost in the place—too meek, too small, too withering to be heard.

Lunging forward again, Louis fumbled one of the meal bars when he tried stuffing it into his pocket. It hit the ground and was kicked away by another patron. Louis didn't notice. He was moving faster now.

Behind him, a security guard called out in a crackling voice, "Sir, hold on."

Louis didn't hear the kid. People were gasping now and laughing and jeering, and Clyde's voice boomed above it all, "I cannot be barred! I will not be!"

Through a collapsing gap in the lobby, Louis caught a glimpse of Lydia's face. She looked stricken; her complexion gone to ash.

Skidding under the velvet rope in the center of the lobby, Louis popped up again just in time to catch Clyde's big, dumb head and his giant, rounded shoulders bustling into the entrance of the museum. A chorus of shrieks erupted once he'd disappeared from sight. Louis tacked left, following Clyde's direction and fumbling the other meal bar in his hurry.

Behind him, the security guard shouted, "Hey, you! Stop!"

Louis charged past the ticket taker, slipping into the narrow gash Clyde had cut through the crowd. Ahead, women were screaming. Men yapped, thrown aside by the giant.

The tear in the crowd was healing itself, working closed and so Louis led with a shoulder and a blustery string of apologies. Between his yowls of "Excuse me!" and "Sorry!" he managed to lift his head and call out, "Clyde! Clyde, stop!" and when that failed, he yelled, "Fredric!" It made no difference. The man continued stampeding forward, the sightless eyes of a dozen Jackalope staring on.

Just in tow behind Louis, the security guard was still shrieking, but there was so much commotion in the place now,

his voice was just another instrument in the cacophony. An unremarkable baying in the din.

Beyond Clyde, the Bigfoot at the far end of the museum was finally in sight, lit in an angelic glow—it's tufted fur sparkling.

It was clear that Clyde had seen it. The man barreled forward more urgently, his voice rumbling through the museum, "What have you done?! You monsters! What have you done?!"

Louis was closing in on the giant but, closer to the exhibit, the crowd was packed tighter, and so he gave up his excuses, abandoning apologies in favor of moving more aggressively, pushing people when he needed to, knocking one man down in the process. The crowd gasped.

"Hey! Stop!" a dwindling voice called from behind Louis.

Louis barely heard. Clyde was almost in reach now.

"Clyde! Clyde! Fredric!" He reached out to snatch the tail of the man's coat. It was too late. With a flap of the tail, it whipped out from Louis's grasp as the man dropped to his knees, skidding forward, sobbing openly before the giant, stuffed Sasquatch.

The crowd, seeing Clyde coming, had rushed out of the way, clearing a big stage for his performance and now the obligatory cell phones were out, catching the spectacle; everyone filming just in time for Louis to enter the opening, just in time for the security guard to catch up, bombing into frame, snaring Louis around the waist. The two men spilled across the floor.

Oblivious to the wrestling match which had commenced just beside him, Clyde wept into his hands, unbothered by Louis's voice, grunting through barred teeth, "What are you doing, you idiot? Get off of me!"

LET INTO A CELL, Louis was seized with a moment of panic, irrationally imaging the police had deposited him in a bear's cage. Filling up a whole corner of the cinderblock dungeon, the other man in the holding pen was so large, he would have made Clyde look minuscule, if Clyde had been there. Clyde was not there, though. Even as the catalyst for the chaos in the museum, Whitethunder had somehow avoided detention. It was a wellspring of fury for Louis, that is, until he was let into the cell—then, his only concern became the behemoth in the corner.

Slouching, with his head hanging to the side, so that he seemed asleep, when Louis crossed the floor, the man started growling from the back of his throat—Louis could feel the vibrations of it in his chest. Creeping to the furthest bench from the man, Louis sat, pressing himself against the wall.

At Louis's strained stillness, the rumbling in the man's throat subsided. Only when a string of spittle ran from the giant's mouth into his thick, black beard and he commenced snoring, did Louis relax, sliding down the wall a few inches.

After some time, the snoring was interrupted by a deputy arriving at the bars. "Chief wants you."

The giant on the bench grunted something incomprehensible and moved to stand.

"Not you. Sit down, Stan. You—the shoplifter; the uppity one."

Louis ground his teeth and went to the cell door, keeping a weary check on the beast in the corner.

After being led through the cramped inner offices of the Evany P.D., Louis was ushered through a door with a placard that read, 'Captain Conner.'

Inside, Conner was at his desk, looking relaxed, smiling as Louis entered. The deputy was excused, and the door closed at Louis's back. Motioning across his desk to an empty seat, Conner said, "Please, sit."

Everything in the room, from the cheap laminate desk separating the men, to the stamped-metal fan sitting on the file cabinet, seemed from a bygone era. Glistening with pomade, even Alan Conner's hair looked to be on loan from a museum of midcentury fashion.

It was impossible for Louis not to feel imperiled here; too easy to imagine whatever slipshod excuse could be invented to explain how bruises might appear on his face, how he might end up dead.

So as not to succumb to the paralysis of fear, when Louis sat, he put on a heavy frown and aimed it at the cop. Better to be bold. Best to make the man think that the shaking of Louis's hand was all anger, rather than anxiety. He spoke from the bottom of his chest, when he said, "I wasn't read my Miranda's. But, just so you know—I would like my attorney."

"Relax, Price. There aren't gonna be charges. This was clearly just a mixup."

The tightness in Louis's chest lessened, but his scowl settled deeper. "The demand stands."

"The security guard said he saw some items fall from your person. Given your hurry, he assumed they'd been stolen. Not an unreasonable suspicion."

"Given my hurry, or given my race?"

"It was an honest mistake, Price. Best let it go."

"Best for whom?"

"Everyone. All of us."

"*Us*? You know, I've never been arrested before. Never been put in cuffs. Do you know how rare that is for a man of color?"

"You weren't arrested, Price. You were brought in. You're being released. There won't be anything on your record. Like I said, this was all a mixup."

"That's hardly the point."

The man on the other side of the desk just shrugged.

"My person purchased those items. My person would very much like those items returned." Louis stared at the cop. The man stared back, unpersuaded, unimpressed. "My person is goddamned starving!"

The chief leaned aside, drawing open a drawer. When he flipped a meal bar across the desk, Louis caught it. It was not the brand Louis had purchased in the museum gift shop. He was too hungry to make a point of it. Tearing into the package, he gnawed off the end.

"Just relax," Conner said. "I just wanted the opportunity, while you're here, to speak with you."

"You say it was an honest mistake, but to my mind even mistakes have consequences. And your deputies, when they brought me in? Even after I'd explained the situation? Even when I told them to look at the receipt in my pocket? I did have a receipt."

"They said you were belligerent."

"Wouldn't you have been?"

"You've been given apologies."

"I don't believe I have."

"Well, you can have them now."

"Fine." Louis stared at the man. "Say what you gotta say, then, so I can leave."

The cop nodded and tapped a little rhythm out on the desk with the end of his pen, held between his fingers like a cigarette. He said, "I'm curious, why're you here? This 'story' you're working on..." He shook his head. "It doesn't wash."

"I don't know what you're getting at."

"When I saw you at the museum—when you had that attack, I had this feeling about you. Cops, we get feelings like that sometimes, like when we meet someone and just know our paths are gonna cross again."

"Are you trying to tell me I don't belong? Is that what this is? You want me outta your town." Louis chewed on the meal bar with the round, onerous jaw work of a steer, and glared at the cop.

"Not at all." The man shook his head. "Why I wanted to speak with you: I could understand you coming out here if you had a real story to follow—something serious to investigate. Let me tell you, Louis, there are some real stories out here."

"I preferred 'Mr. Price'."

The Captain nodded past Louis's shoulder, toward the closed door. "Stan's would be a good one. You see, the thing is, you're wrong. I do want you here. I do. I think you could do some good here, for the community."

"I'm curious, what exactly was it that you learned about me that makes you think I give a damn about your community?"

"You must think I'm some sort of *Right World* Newsy... No. I'm a cop. I'm trained to see through an act. I meant the *Sentinel* articles. I lived in Seattle, before I got the job out here. Now, the *Sentinel* was always a touch too liberal for my personal tastes, but I liked your work there. I'd forgotten about it until I looked you up, to be honest. But, you're clearly a strong writer, and it seems wasted on that dumb internet show. I don't know, maybe a bigger waste than your chasing hokum all around the Peninsula, though it's a close call..."

"Okay," Louis said after swallowing the last bite of the meal bar. He wadded up the empty wrapper and placed it on the desktop. It slowly uncurled itself. Louis crossed his arms over his chest and said, "Fine. Tell me about Stan, so I can get on with my life."

The man smiled a mechanical smile. "I was hoping you'd see it my way. Where to begin?" The Chief looked around the ceiling for a moment before returning his attention to Louis, "I guess I'd begin with Stan's father, or maybe his grandfather, even."

"...My hopes of this story being succinct are for naught, huh?"

Conner ignored him. "Stan's grandfather was a lumber-jack, a man who worked the forest. Like all men of that kind, he worked very hard for very little. He worked hard so that his family, his sons and daughters, could have a better shot at the American dream. He worked so that they'd have a route away from the kind of work he had to do all his life. He wanted to make sure that they had the luxury of staying in school as long as they needed, so they could learn as much as they needed and have that knowledge as a bedrock on which to build their own futures."

"Sounds like you've got this story written already."

The cop ignored him, kept talking. "It would have worked, too, if Stan's father hadn't been so stubborn as to want to do exactly the kind of work that his father did. So, when Stan's father's brothers and sisters quit the area in search of greener financial pastures, Stan's father stayed on, working the forest, ignorant that what he was doing wasn't in keeping with his old man's actual wishes.

"By the time Stan came along, and grew up, the poor dope considered forestry his birthright. His father'd been a lumber-jack and his grandfather. Who can blame the guy for wanting to continue a tradition?

"So, Stan gets a job with the same outfit that his father works. The two of them work side by side for years.

"In that time, Stan gets married, has a son of his own. Time moves on, as time will, and Stan and his father fell tree after tree and Stan's son grows and eventually time fells Stan's father. Actually, I think it was a logging accident which felled Stan's father, but in the end, it's the same. Loggers don't live long and something was bound to fell that man sooner or later.

"Well, in the absence of Stan's father, Stan carries on. He continues working the forest, one tree at a time. I guess that man would have kept it up until he followed his father off the edge of the living world, but somebody else happened to die first: a woman name of Evelyn Langhorn. There's no reason, not being from around here, that you'd know the name, unless you happen to be familiar with the Evelyn S. Langhorn Land Trust. Here's the deal; Evelyn passes. She's the last in her family. She has no heirs, no living relations at all. Her will stipulates that all her assets are to be auctioned off and all the proceeds are to be placed in a foundation to benefit," he flitted his hand dismissively, "various cultural things or whatnot. The land that Stan's grandfather, his father and Stan himself had worked goes up for auction. The government buys that land, names it after that dead old lady and folds it into the national park. The thinking, I guess, was that there was a sad lack of public land out on the Peninsula. I don't know what fool did that math. But, there it is."

Louis was silent, staring dully.

"You know what happens when a man losses his livelihood, Price? He losses himself, his sense of purpose. He becomes like a ship without a captain, unmoored, drifting about.

"Stan tries getting work with another outfit but that land going to the Fed has created a shortage of workable land and a glut of loggers. So, the only reasonable option is unemployment. Problem is, Stan's real stubborn. He's the kind of man raised to look down on welfare, right or wrong. See, he thinks there's gotta be another way.

"Truth is: right now, there's only one industry expanding on the Peninsula. You know what that is?"

Louis kept silent, though he could have ventured a guess and would have been right.

"The illicit drug trade. Meth, heroin. Now, Stan isn't a druggie, but for a man of his stature, he's got a specific usefulness to someone moving contraband. Mostly, he thinks, he's been hired on for his looks, his size. He falls in with a group of boys, a biker gang, distributing. He goes to deals, looks stern and that's about it, and about all Stan ever expected. Of course, that kinda job doesn't last. Eventually, a man in that trade has to act.

So he does. He hurts some people, because he has to. He hurts them and in doing that he hurts himself, he injures his soul doing that."

"So sad, what can happen to nice, white folk," Louis intoned flatly.

"Well, he's finally making money. Not a lot, 'cause, honestly, unless you're EL Chapo, nobody makes money in the drug trade: the margins are thin, the risks high.

"So, even though he's finally making money enough to put food on his family's table, he's not really making enough to do much else. Not enough to keep up with the house, which is starting to fall apart. Not enough to fill the oil tank which is bad, 'cause there's another winter on the way. But, by this time, Stan's real seasoned in getting by. He's been doing it for years. His father left him property and that property is wooded, and even though he's a little outta practice, he is still a trained lumberjack. So he fells trees. He chops wood. He gets ready for winter and they're certain to make it through another season and surely things will get better after that. Things are starting to get strained with him and his wife. She wanted a man with a man's job, not this... What he's fallen into. You see, I know things were strained, because I got called up to his house a few times.

"Anyhow, Stan's out late one night, making a deal and when he gets home, he's terrified by the emergency lights flashing up near his house. It's a raid. It must be. He's caught, but he's too piss-scared to deal with it right then. He turns his truck around and bombs out to Port Angeles and takes a room in a dive motel to try and wait it out. He's there days, expecting that, at any moment, someone's gonna come busting in his door, to haul him off to jail.

"That knock never comes. He starts to get lonely. He misses his wife and kid and so he thinks he oughta just go home.

"Thing is, there's no home anymore where his home used to stand. When he pulls into the driveway, he sees his house is burned right to the ground, just the king studs of his front door left standing, looking like a pair of burnt matchsticks stuck in the dirt. Stan turns his truck right around and comes racing into town, right to this very police station.

"He wants to know what happened." The Captain shrugged. "What happened? There was a chimney fire on account of the chimney not being swept for years. His wife and his son are both gone.

"Now, I told you what happens when a man loses his livelihood. When a man loses his family?" Conner shook his head lowly. "He's gone. Any hold society may have had on him. It's gone. He's an animal, fit for little more than solitude, wilderness living...

"So, you may look at him and see an animal or a monster, you may see something without a soul at all. But you gotta know what took his soul from him. And you gotta know, that this Peninsula is chock full of Stans. I pull Stans in every goddamned day. It's not just the junkies, it's everyone. The whole community. You see, Stan may never have been a saint, but when he had a stake, at least he could be a citizen. Now? He's got nothing and that's the most dangerous kind of man there is.

"And nobody cares about them. Instead, we get news crews filling up the parking lot of some bullshit tourist-trap museum... I'll tell you, I've never seen a Bigfoot. I've lived in the Pacific Northwest my whole life, and I've never seen a Bigfoot. Stans? They're everywhere and they're dying. And they're killing each other. And they're tearing this community apart. And it has to stop. And for it to stop, people need to start paying attention. That's where you come in. Because I think you could help with that, Louis. It's a real story, and it's a heartbreaker, and it needs to be put in front of people."

The room fell to silence. After a moment, Louis said, "I'm sorry—what exactly is it you expect me to do?"

"You write. Write about it. You're in the industry—get people involved. Shit, I don't know what you do, but whatever it is, do it! Once the public sees this—once they really see it—they'll start demanding action..."

"I'm sorry, this isn't news, Conner. The public knows. All of America knows..."

"Then why isn't anyone acting?"

"Because they've made the calculation. Stan isn't worth the effort. He's disposable. You said it yourself, no one cares."

"That's your job: you make them care."

Louis scoffed and shook his head. "That's not my job. My job is providing whatever it is people want. That's my job: creating a product to sate an appetite. That's my job. This? People don't want this. It's depressing. People want their beliefs reinforced, or a distraction. It's hard to see that there's anything beyond that that people want." Louis looked at the man across the table dully for a moment. "Besides, why should anyone care one iota about someone like Stan? So much bemoaning the slow suicide of a bunch of hillbillies. I have my own problems. Stan made his choice. Why should anybody care? Why should I even care?"

Conner bobbed his head. He said, "Because you side with the underdog."

Louis glowered at Conner and said, "See, the thing is, Stan doesn't sound like an underdog to me. He seems like another entitled white man, who squandered his own advantages. Can I leave now? Am I free to go?"

He'd already risen from his chair.

Conner's expression fell. Rather than say it, he gestured to the door, turning from Louis to shuffle some paperwork on his desk.

Louis let himself out.

TRAILED BY A UNIFORMED escort out of the back offices of the police station, Louis was released into the lobby. Spotting Lydia and Clyde there, waiting for him, he turned sharply away.

The pair on the bench must have thought Louis simply hadn't seen them: rising to their feet, they hurried forward, only stopping when Louis whipped around. Holding out the palm of his hand, he said, "No."

Clearing his throat, Clyde started to respond.

"No," Louis insisted more forcefully, cutting the man quiet. He turned and pushed through the doors.

Outside, the wind blowing down the street was clammy and cold and Louis could blame it for the wetness in the corners of his eyes. The sidewalk was empty.

He felt like a child again—drowning in the same loneliness he'd been immersed in on his grandfather's farm—stuck in the barn, watching the rain come down.

What *was* he doing? Conner was right: this wasn't a story, it wasn't a real story at all. The most authentic thing about it was a Swede with boxed black hair claiming to be descendant of an animal no one had any proof of. The whole thing was a falsehood, top to bottom. In the back of Louis's mind, there dawned a sudden aching loneliness. He needed Maria. How long had it been since they'd last spoken? Since he'd been in Port Angeles, days ago. But he couldn't call. He knew that. Not now. What would he even say? All he knew was that he needed to return home. He needed to get off the Peninsula and back to civilization. Good old, broken civilization...

At least the motel wasn't far. He could already see the second floor balcony, just beyond the next rise of buildings.

Back in his room, Louis threw everything into his suitcase, and stood immobile, staring at it. Splayed open, both halves were mounded higher than the clasps. Closing the top, when he gave the zipper a hard tug, it wouldn't budge. Pulling the bag to the edge of the bed he sat on it, forcing it down with his weight.

He was sweaty and his hands were trembling by the time he got the zipper closed up, and he laughed at his success—a mad, joyless laugh.

Yanking the suitcase from the bed, he only made it three paces toward the door, before a great tearing sound announced the surrender of the seams. The bag came open, disgorging itself across the floor.

Swearing and tossing the bag away, Louis stood, shaking with frustration.

His jaw was still clenched tight when he met Lydia on the staircase from the motel's second floor balcony, his suitcase held before him, lashed closed by two belts, fastened together end to end and looped around the girth.

Lydia frowned at the strapping before turning her attention to him. "Louis, I understand you're upset..."

She had to back against the railing so he could pass. He didn't seem like he intended to slow.

After he'd stormed by, she fell in line behind him, trailing him down the stairs and across the parking lot to the Benz. Rain had washed away the bulk of the mud, but the front bumper was unaligned, a crooked smile aimed at the ground.

"I understand you're angry, Louis."

"Oh, thank you, Lydia, that's very validating." He didn't turn, he didn't slow. The trunk of the car popped open and he lobbed his suitcase inside, slamming the trunk closed again and marching around to the driver's door.

"Louis, can we please just talk about what happened at the museum?"

"No need to talk. It is what it is. It happens to black men every day. Nothing significant."

"That isn't what I'm talking about, Louis... Louis, I found our hunters."

LOUIS TURNED BACK. From the third floor balcony, there was clear view of the parking lot behind the apartment building. Only one vehicle sat down there—a pickup truck with three different colors of side paneling and an American flag banner covering the back window. The sight of it set Louis ill-at-ease. He knew the kind of man that applied that sort of decal to a window, and had been callused by a lifetime of interactions with such men.

Turning back to the door, though the shades were drawn, in the gloomy day, the light inside could be seen—warm and filthy, the hue of mucus on a tissue.

It took awhile for someone to come to the door. Long enough, in fact, so that Lydia managed another burst of drumming on it in the moments before it did open.

Beyond the gap was a woman in jeans and a camisole threadbare enough so that little of her body was secret. She had a large tattoo—maybe it was a birthmark—on one hip. On the opposite hip, she cradled a pale, blonde child. Her eyes were clear and cold, two hole-punches of autumn sky.

Briefly looking back and forth between Lydia and Louis, she said nothing to either. Leaving the door wide, she turned, barking into the apartment, "Corey, those folks here for you."

The hallway ended in a spare, open-use room, a kitchenette half-filled one wall. In a lopsided recliner in the corner of the room, a man sat, just as light of hair and complexion as the pair who'd answered the door. On his knee sat an olive skinned boy with tight, black curls all over his head. Somehow, Louis instantly felt himself come unwound a few turns. That little, brown-skinned boy was like the canary in the mine, letting Louis know he needn't fear—at least not as much as he otherwise would have.

"Howdy." The man in the chair nodded at the couch, and Lydia and Louis sat.

"Thanks for meeting with me again, Corey. This is Louis Price. We really appreciate you taking the time," Lydia said as she worked a small pad of paper and a pen from the inside pocket of her coat.

"Do you mind if I record?" Louis asked, reaching into his own jacket for his phone.

"I'd prefer you not."

Louis just had the phone pinched between his fingers. He let it go. It slid back down to the basin of his pocket, tugging at the fabric when it landed. He nodded. "I understand. Handsome kid. Neighbor's?" Louis asked. He could feel Lydia tense beside him.

"This is my son," the man in the recliner said. "From another... Well, it isn't important. Say hi, Earl."

The boy mouthed the word hello before turning quickly, burying his face in the man's chest, hiding a little smile dimpling his round cheeks.

Lydia said, "So, we'd like to hear about how you bagged the animal in Marcus Auster's museum."

"First of all, I want it known, I wasn't a part of that."

"Outside the museum, you told me..." Lydia started to say. She was quickly cut off by the man in the recliner. He'd started rocking anxiously, the springs of the seat squawking.

"I didn't have anything to do with killing the damned thing." Corey adjusted the boy on his lap. "Okay. I'm in bed, right? Sleeping. It's quarter past two or something—some ungodly hour. The phone rings. I look and see, it's Tom Morrow. Shoot. I almost didn't answer. He likes to drink, you know. It's far from the first time he's called me like that. But I didn't want it waking the kids. He," Corey shrugged, "doesn't sound drunk.

But he's real excited. He keeps saying, 'I bagged one! I bagged one!' and I'm like, 'What are you talking about?' and he says he shot himself a Bigfoot. I didn't even answer that. Just hung up. Shit."

The woman at the sink said, "Corey," so softly, Louis barely heard her.

"Right. Sorry, babe." He ran his free hand through his hair before returning his attention to Louis and Lydia and continuing, "He calls back and I send it to voicemail and turn off the ringer and shut my eyes, but the light from the phone starts going off and the thing's buzzing and Dianne jabs me, like it's my fault, and I'm like, he's just not gonna let me sleep, so I pick up. Go out in the hall. He's still excited, I can tell, but now he's talking real insistent, saying I need to come over, he needs my help 'cause he can't move the thing himself. He's says there's gonna be money. A lot of money. I've heard that from him before, so I tell him, if I'm coming out, I want a hundred bucks for it in hand—he can keep his 'cut'..."

"So you go?" Lydia asked.

"Right. I go. His truck is parked off this logging road, I don't know, mile from his house. I get out. There's no sign of him. I start calling out into the woods. Don't hear anything back. Okay. Fine. He's drunk, I guess, but I already came all that way out and so I get out my phone, give him call. He tells me he's out on a trail, a quarter mile from the road and can I please hurry up. I'm pretty annoyed, pretty sure I'm gonna find him out in the woods shitty..."

"Corey."

"Sorry, hon... It'd snowed that day, up in those heights. The land's covered with this thin layer of slush and I can see his foot prints, melted through the slush, black in the night. I follow the path, and I find him, just as he said, quarter mile or so out. As I suspected, he is drunk.

"But he does have something. Hard to tell. Looks like a bear, maybe. It was real dark. There's this big patch of ground around the thing that's all black from him having stepped around it, trying to get it moved on his own."

"You said, you thought it was a bear?"

"It was real dark and the thing was big. I dunno. I wasn't about to hop right on board his Sasquatch story, or whatever."

"You didn't bring a flashlight?"

"Nope. All that slush on the ground made it easy enough to see. Of course, now I wish I had brought one, 'cause I didn't get a good look at the thing. Anyhow, crouched down on the ground beside the thing with a bottle of Grandpa between his legs, Tommy just looks up at me grinning. 'Look,' he says, 'I bagged one. I told you.'" All the chest-rumbling talk had upset the boy and he fussed, slid off Corey's lap and toddled across the room. Louis watched him move behind the couch. The woman who'd answered the door was standing, looking silently out the window over the sink and the boy trundled up to her and wrapped his arms around her leg. She set her free hand on his head. Her other arm was still slung under the child lodged on her narrow hip.

Corey said, "Well, I guess it'd been awhile since that phone call to my house because he's really dug into that bottle by now. I tell him, 'That's a bear you bagged, you dumb hick,' but he just argues with me over it. Anyhow, I take a few pulls off the bottle, on account the night is cold and I'm out in the woods, woken up by this dumb son of a..."

"...Corey..."

"...Sorry. So, it's a ways back and this—whatever it is he bagged—weighs like a ton. It musta been four hundred pounds, at least and we're just dragging it through the woods. It's hard work. We'll drag the thing for ten yards and then we stop, panting. Pass the bottle a bit, start dragging again. So, by the time we're finally back at the logging road, he can barely stand, and I'm pretty lit up, too. It's a struggle getting that damned animal up in the back of his pickup, lemme tell you. It's like trying to lift a trash bag full of shi—"

"Corey!"

"Sorry, baby..." Corey paused and cleared his throat. "Finally, we get 'er in and he says, you know, follow him to his house so I can offload the thing. Okay. So we're not even driving for a half a minute before old Tommy starts swerving and—bam!—runs off the road, right into a culvert. So, okay—hell! I pull over. His airbags are blown out. His nose is bleeding. He's just laughing his ass off. I'm like, okay, drunk-o, you wrecked your damned truck so come on and I'll give you a ride home, but he won't leave the animal, so I gotta back up to his truck and we slide it from his bed to mine and then we get on the road again. So, we finally land back at his place and get under the lights—it's bright as a day on the beach, there, he's got these big halogen lamps all around his dooryard—so I can finally see the thing, figure out if it's a bear or not, but now, I don't know if it was him smashing the truck into that culvert or if he shot the thing in its damned face, but I still can't tell what it is. It's just bloodied up. Smushed up. A mess. So, who knows?" Corey shrugged. "That's it, mostly. We dragged it back to the shed he uses for dressing animals and, yeah, that's it."

Lydia was shaking her head, her face a constellation of creases. "But you couldn't tell if it was a bear or not? Not definitively? What about the paws? What about the arms?"

"I dunno. I never thought to look at the paws, I guess. By the time we got back there, into the light, I was pretty drunk and tired and just wanted to be back in bed. I dunno. I guess the arms seemed longer than I would have expected, the legs, too. But I've never seen a real bear up close, either. They keep away."

"They're smart," Louis said.

"That's right."

"Did you think, by the time you got back there," Lydia said, "were you still thinking it was a bear, or were you more convinced that it was... Something else"

"I dunno. I thought it was a bear the whole time, I guess. Like I said, Tommy was really drunk."

"So, what was he doing out in the woods, hunting?"

"Well, he told me about that later. He said this thing had been coming around his property for a few nights, making these awful calls. He said he started tracking it, just out of curiosity and said that he found what seemed to be its primary territory, out off that logging road and figured, if he could bag it, there was no limit to what Marcus Auster would pay for the thing. Turns out, he was wrong about that last part, there was definitely a limit."

"Yeah?"

"Yeah. He short-changed us, I know it. That son of a bitch is gonna make a fortune. But, he told us, because Tommy stuffed it, rather than leaving it intact, it just wasn't worth much. So, Tommy says he'd happily deliver the innards of the thing but Auster just rolls his eyes at that. Too late, he says."

"So, you saw it after Tommy had done the taxidermy?"

"Oh, yeah. We delivered it together. That was part of what Tommy ended up giving me a cut for. And being quiet."

"How much was your cut?" Louis asked.

"Twenty percent. Little over two grand."

Lydia asked, "And what did you think when you saw it stuffed, in daylight."

Corey shrugged. "Looked like a Bigfoot. More than any bear, I guess."

She asked, "Do you think your friend Tommy had the skill as a taxidermist to make the corpse of a bear look like the thing you delivered to Marcus Auster?"

"First of all, Tommy's not my friend, not really. He was a friend of my father's..."

"But, do you think he was capable?"

"I don't know. Maybe. He swore up and down that it was a Bigfoot and I've never known him to be the kind of man who'd lie like that. He could embellish with the best of them, but mostly, in my experience, his stories were rooted in truth.

"Plus, something kidnapped him."

"Kidnapped? What do you mean kidnapped?" Louis said.

"Well. It'd been over a week since I'd heard anything from Tommy and normally if that sorta span goes on and I haven't heard anything from the old drunk, I'll call him just to check in or whatever. I call. No answer. A few more days go by and I don't hear anything. I decide I oughta go check on his place. The house is fine. Locked up and dark. I know where he keeps a spare key, so I go inside. I'm half expecting to find him dead in there. You know, every corner I turn I kinda got my eyes squinted like maybe I'll come across something I don't really wanna see. He isn't anywhere inside. So, I'm back in the kitchen, kinda looking around casually and I see the door to his barn's open—torn free, standing beside the barn, lodged in the ground and kind of tugging in the wind. I go out there. It's empty, but there are these giant footprints all around the shed, and leading out to the woods. So I figure, you know—this is gonna sound crazy," Corey said and shook his head and stopped talking.

The dark-haired boy had come back around, standing at Corey's feet with his arms up-stretched. The man bent and picked up the boy with a grunt and let the boy settle in his lap.

"Go ahead and say it," Lydia said.

Still, Corey kept mum until the boy had settled, looking out at the two strangers, coyly from his father's arms. "I dunno, I guess I surmised some relative of that Bigfoot had come around and snatched Tommy. Like, for vengeance or whatever. I'd heard stories like that when I was a kid."

"You call the police?"

"Weird coincidence. They happened to show up while I was out there. Neighbors, I guess, had gotten worried, too, that they hadn't seen Tommy around."

"What'd the police do?"

Corey shrugged. "I'd say a lotta nothing."

"Did you tell them about that night, about the Bigfoot."

Corey shook his head. "No. I'm worried about what could happen to me. What could happen to my family if people knew about it. Plus, there really is no reason to think the two incidents were related. I did show the cop the prints I found. I said, 'What do you think makes a print that looks like that?' He did not have much of an answer." Corey shrugged. "They were all full of water and pretty indistinct looking. Just melting away in the rain and I could tell he didn't see anything in them at all. But, I did what I needed to do, so now it's his responsibility, I guess. I mean, if it hadn't been for me going out that night to help Tommy, I probably wouldn't have seen them as tracks, either."

On their way out, in the parking lot, Corey Dibiase let down the tailgate of his pickup truck, so that Louis and Lydia could see where the corpse had lain. Louis had barely started to examine the fitted plastic liner, when Lydia grabbed his arm excitedly.

"There! There, Louis," she pointed.

Snagged between the liner and the wall of the bed, was a little tuft of fur.

TOM MORROW'S HOUSE wasn't visible from the street.

Tom Morrow's house could barely be seen from directly in front of Tom Morrow's house. Vines climbed the telephone poles lining the driveway, where the lights Corey Dibiase had described were mounted. Overgrown shrubs buried the facade. All that was visible of the home was the cinderblock chimney, and it gave the impression that there was a destitute family of elves occupying those unkempt bushes. The half-circle driveway was the only place within sight that wasn't surrendered to weeds and overgrowth—and even there, a scraggly mohawk of grass ran the center, tickling the trailer hitch of the aged pickup plugging up the exit.

Lydia killed the engine of the 4Runner and she and Louis sat, staring out at the clog of wilderness that had filled in the land. Beyond the shrub-house, the roof of a barn peaked out above a tangle of evergreen boughs.

"It looks like nobody's been here in ages," Lydia said, when they stepped out, into the driveway.

The grille and the drivers-side fender of Tom Morrow's truck were both crumpled. The driver's side headlamp was missing—an empty eye-socket staring out at the world. Louis and Lydia shared a look. Neither one spoke.

Turning to examine the clog of vines in the backyard, Lydia said, "You think that's the barn where Corey found the footprints?"

"If not that barn, some other death-trap back there."

It took some searching to access the backyard; the driveway was bordered by a mess of overgrowth as tall and impenetrable as the shrubs before the house, if less homogeneous. Somewhere between the tailgate of the pickup and the hidden corner of the house, there was a well-trod hole; too narrow for them to enter side-by-side. Louis led.

Past the wall of overgrowth, the property opened up, but only superficially. The path widened so a pair could walk abreast, but beyond the parameters of the pathway, the wilderness had flooded in like a tide. The roofs of a few rust-brown vehicles poked from the tangle, vines closing over the tops, as though trying to drag those old hunks underground. The path snaked lazily, passing inaccessible outbuildings, cordoned off and overcome with vines. The door of one of the sheds was bound open with an infestation of creepers. Deep, deep darkness peered out from inside.

Ahead, the boughs of the trees separated as Lydia and Louis drew nearer the barn. A patch of limp grass beside the path had somehow not been overtaken, and so Louis stepped off the path, coming wide of the barn, to get a better look, stopping, so suddenly it drew Lydia's attention. She halted as well.

"What is it?" she whispered.

Louis laughed awkwardly. His normal tone seemed boorishly loud when he said, "Nothing," and shook his head.

Lydia was still looking at him.

"My grandfather. My mother's father. He had a barn like that. I mean, not like that. He wouldn't have let it go like that. But, you know, it was just like that, with that high hay door." Louis raised his gaze up a little higher. "The same roof, with that kind of pitch." Louis pointed, tracing the pitch with his finger.

"A gambrel roof."

"That's right. A gambrel roof. I used to spend summers there."

"On his farm? That must have been nice."

Louis shook his head. "No. In the barn. When I was young, my mother didn't like leaving me home alone. So, I had to spend my summers at her father's house. If it was nice weather, I was outside. And if it was raining, I stayed in the barn with the dogs.

"The last summer I spent there, it rained for weeks. I was in the barn with the dogs nearly every day. I begged my mother to let me stay home. She just told me I was too young.

"This one, particularly rainy day I'm in there with the dogs and I get an emergency. It's raining so hard, I can barely see my grandfather's house through the sheets of rain. I try to hold on, but at a certain point it just became obvious that that strategy wasn't going to last. Finally, I go out the side door of the barn and, under the eves, take care of business. Well, at the end of the day my mother comes and picks me up and that's that.

"But, the next day's sunny and warm, when my mother drops me off. I go into the barn to set down my lunch bag and she drives away and the moment she's gone, I see 'Mr. Price' coming out of his house. I don't know how I knew it, but I knew: I'd been caught. He comes to the barn door and gestures for me to come out of the shadows. So, I come out. He leads me around the backside of the barn. There, sitting on the ground is a turd and it's half flattened and there's the tread of a boot printed in it, so I know that he stepped in my shit, and it's hard not smiling at that. I wanna smile, but mostly I'm terrified.

"I tried to blame the dogs. He didn't buy it, said the dogs had the civility to shit in the woods. I got a beating that day.

"Never did have to go back to that barn, though. Next morning, my mother tells me, 'I think you were right, Louis. I think you're old enough to stay home alone.' I still don't know whether it was my own mother taking pity on me, or if it was my grandfather telling her he wouldn't have me. I never saw that man again."

"Jesus, Louis. That's an awful story."

Louis shrugged. "I always thought it was a good story. Good ending, anyway. After that, I was just at home during the summers. I'd go for bike rides and stuff, but I don't know—I became kind of obsessed with my mother's closet. I'd found one of your books in there, by accident and I guess I sort of convinced myself that there were clues in that closet about my father, and I just had to work out how it all connected, and then I'd be able to figure out who he was. I dunno. I guess your book led me to think that finding answers was always possible—that answers were out there, waiting to be found..."

Louis shrugged again and started forward, but stopped suddenly when Lydia's hand caught the arm of his jacket. He turned to her. She was staring at his feet, her face pale. Louis followed the direction of her gaze.

Just before him (he would have hit it dead center with his next footstep) was a rusty bear trap, its nubby brown teeth aimed at the sky, the jaws open wide as can be.

Slowly, Lydia released her grip.

"You think it would have closed?" Louis's head had gone light, a sheen of sweat materializing on his forehead despite the cold of the day.

"I don't think I want to find out. Do you think..." Lydia didn't finish the thought.

The barn door had been torn free, but it was impossible to tell if it was just a natural symptom of the blight of neglect that had infested the property, or if 'something' had torn it free. Inside the open mouth of the barn it was a mess of darkness, gray wood and cobwebs. At the corner of the barn, another trap could be seen, half-hiding under a pile of leaves. There was no telling how many more there might be, but the yard suddenly felt littered with them—danger in every potential step.

"In light of the traps," Lydia said, "I propose we not go wandering any further."

"I second the motion."

Back in the car, they both sat quietly for a moment.

"What do you think?"

"The traps certainly tell of a man in fear." Lydia had a map leaned up against the steering wheel and was going over it, her fingers and eyes wandering along between the folds. "Yup. Look here..."

Louis looked. "What?"

"This is Tom Morrow's property." She stabbed a finger down, and then a second, without moving her hand. "This is Clyde's."

"They're close."

"They're abutting."

Louis scoffed, shook his head. "Kidnapped, by a Sasquatch."

"It's a pretty common theme in Bigfoot stories..."

"Yeah, but..."

"But?"

"I don't know, I always took those stories as bullshit, you know? A pioneer's excuse for a blackout bender..."

"I don't think Tom Morrow laid those traps because he was worried about blacking out."

"No," Louis rubbed the back of his neck. "No, I suppose not."

LOUIS'S NEW BACKPACK had been neutered of its retail tags. He'd left the trashcan beneath the motel desk overflowing with packaging; color-printed cuts of cardboard and empty plastic coffins that had held flashlights and pocket knives, fire starters, a compass: items the wilderness necessitated a man have. He'd sent Maria a text—too early to call (the sun wasn't up when he stepped out onto the balcony)—and'd gone down to the lobby of the Evany Motel to give the clerk at the front desk his room number for the final time.

Outside, in the early morning darkness, Louis had been surprised to find Clyde at the back hatch of Lydia's 4Runner, forcing a bag into the cargo hold. When the man offered Louis a gentle, "Good morning," Louis slid forward, taking Lydia by the arm and directing her to the privacy a few yards of pavement provided.

"What the hell is he doing here?"

"Well, he's coming, of course."

"Why?!"

"Why? To act as a guide—at least in a limited scope. He's familiar with the area, even if one chooses to disregard his purported ancestry."

Louis gave the man a sly appraisal, before returning his attention to Lydia. The giant was still preoccupied, tinkering with the arrangement of bags in the back of the SUV. "Listen, Lydia, I haven't been completely forthcoming with you. The fact is, I did a little investigating of our friend Mr. Whitethunder

over there. You see, there is no such person as Clyde Whitethunder. It's an alias. His name is actually..."

The dissolve of Lydia's expression made Louis's words run
short.

She starred at him a moment, before saying, "I honestly
don't know what I find more insulting, Louis, that you were intentionally withholding information from me, or that you think
so little of my abilities that you'd assume I wouldn't have re-
searched him myself."

Louis stammered a moment. "Well, it sounds like you've
been withholding information from me, too, if you chose not to
tell me, either."

"I didn't tell you, Louis, because I didn't think it was relevant to anything. You, apparently, don't feel the same." With
that she turned from him, and she'd been quiet toward him for
the rest of the morning.

And now, here he was.

Ahead—above him—Lydia and Clyde were still climbing;
their snowshoes whomping in the snow like pillows beaten
against bedding.

Louis paused to look back. In a frame of snow laden boughs,
the white capped forest drew away to where it met with a sky
the color of bruised apple flesh. He moved on again, lagging behind the other two.

The air felt like river pebbles in his throat, in his lungs,
coldness pressing in all around him.

Wisps of snow drifted. It was impossible to determine their
source. It seemed inconceivable that they had come from the
sky; they swayed and wafted parallel with it, even though Louis
could sense no breeze stirring. Setting his feet, he started upward again.

The snowshoes had complicated Louis's whole morning. So
as not to trip, he'd learned to step with his legs bowed unnatu-
rally. His hips and groin ached with the effort. Then, just as he'd
started feeling he'd adapted, they'd come upon this hill. Climbing proved a new kind of challenge; the snowy slope trying to

hold the toe of his snowshoe every time he lifted a leg. Exaggerating each step to clear the incline, he trundled up the sloppy path Clyde had tamped. Now his hips ached, and his abdomen and his ass, and he could already sense the sort of soreness he'd face tomorrow.

At the crest of the hill, the land leveled.

A little distant from Louis, when Lydia and Clyde spoke, their voices seemed like cracks in the otherwise perfect, icy silence. When they were quiet, and Louis paused, all he could hear was the breath of the wilderness—the empty hiss of still air and snow settling.

LOUIS FELT LIKE HE'D traveled a full year of seasons that morning. Before they'd crossed the foothills of the Olympics, he briefly caught the rising sun—peering out through a tear in the clouds. Ten minutes later, the rain resumed.

They'd tromped through mud for an hour, and then through slush for an hour longer. It had frozen to his boots and he sat on the hump of a downed tree, breaking it free with the butt of his pocket knife, before he could strap on the snowshoes and continue.

Now, the snow below his feet was a mystery to be guessed at—it could have been inches deep or yards; there was no telling.

They walked through the morning and broke for lunch, Lydia sitting on her pack, Louis imitating her. She seemed so natural in this winter world, that Louis couldn't help feeling that everything she did, she was doing in just the right way.

Clyde crouched on his snowshoes, jawing a strip of jerky. His pack, Louis surmised, would not have borne the man's weight. Fashioned from one long band of rough deer hide and given shape by a system of sticks and twine, the man had been quiet when Louis asked if it was NorthFace or Eddie Bauer.

For his part, Louis had a project of his own in the form of a meal bar that had gone stiff with cold in his rucksack. His jaw felt done in before he'd softened the first bite enough to swal-

low. He made himself finish it. Afterward, the muscles in his jaw and temples ached. He was still hungry. He took a pair more meal bars from his pack and slipped them inside his coat, hoping his body heat would loosen them. When he'd settled down again, rubbing his sore jaw with a gloved hand, he asked Lydia, "So why this direction?"

They'd long since passed the place where Corey Dibiase claimed to have met with Tom Morrow and, as far as Louis was concerned, any direction after that must have been chosen by some sort of educated guesstimation—some logic earned by Lydia after years of hunting the forest's most elusive inhabitant.

She looked at Louis. Her attention wound slowly to Clyde, until Louis felt he'd no choice but to turn his attention to the giant as well.

Preaching to the tree tops, Clyde said, "I believe there is sign out here. It is my belief that this is the direction from which the creature in the museum was traveling. And, if there is sign, we are certain to find it."

Louis closed his eyes and rubbed his jaw again. "You *believe* there's sign out here?"

"Yes. That is correct. I believe there is sign."

Louis closed his eyes again. "Why?"

"There is an old Klallam tale about a fox who mistakes his shadow for a traveling companion. He is saddened when the winter rains come and his friend disappears. But every Spring, without fail, his companion returns to hunt with him."

Louis stared at the man. "I'm not seeing the connection there, Clyde."

"I have told you how I feel bound to the Sasquatch, how I feel that I am related to her in some way. This feeling I have has led us here, and I believe it will lead us to sign, if not to the creature herself."

"And if there's none?"

"If there is no sign: we will have had a nice walk."

Louis nodded numbly and went quiet.

They started out again, Clyde leading the way.

Falling in beside Lydia, laboring outside the trail Clyde had plowed, Louis said, "We're just following him, huh? That's the plan?"

Lydia shrugged. "You told me your job doesn't require a certain outcome. That the journey is the point."

"We're just following him. The man who got me arrested. If I had known that, I might have saved myself the trip."

She gave Louis a quick, sidelong look. "Clyde didn't get you arrested."

"You gotta be kidding me."

She shrugged. "When a security guard says to stop, Louis..."

"You gotta be kidding me. There're two reasons I was arrested. That man is one of them..." he thrust his finger forward, aimed at Clyde's back. The giant trundled on dumbly, deafened by the crunch of snow beneath his weight.

Lydia sighed. "Michael always said the younger generation was too quick to blame every circumstance on race..."

"Oh, did he?"

She only shrugged again.

Louis fell silent and slowed, and Lydia pulled away. He watched her go.

After a few moments, he stepped into her trail and continued on again, leaving a long breadth between her snowshoes and his own.

The land descended into a valley basin, clear of the high, black canopy of Douglas Firs they'd been sheltered by all morning. Scattered with aspens as straight and regular as two-by-fours, and so evenly spaced it seemed their arrangement had been designed, the sky, rippled and downy, was visible through the gnarled, naked branches. Wisps of snow fell, white specks against the gray.

THEY MADE CAMP at the edge of the aspens and ate dinner in the early evening beneath a pink ribboned sky. It seemed improbable that the sun might be responsible for the color; the day had been overcast since sunup.

After dinner, Lydia melted snow in her camp pot for tea. A staggering amount of it was needed to make a pot full of water—it must have been ten pots worth of snow, before there was enough water for three modest cups of tea.

Clyde yammered on throughout the meal and Louis ignored the man. But then, full of reconstituted, freeze-dried beef stew, the giant'd gone silent. In the opening, Louis asked Lydia, "What if it was just a bear?"

"That time of year, at that elevation, you'd expect a bear to have either hibernated or moved on to somewhere warmer and more fruitful. That doesn't rule out a bear, but I'd say it makes a bear less likely as the culprit," she said and stood, bringing the pot to his outstretched cup. It was the same vessel that had held his beef stew and, even though he'd scrubbed it with a handful of snow, little pearls of grease swirled to the surface with the tea.

The question had obviously drawn Whitethunder's attention; he looked at Lydia as she made her round to him. "Oh," she must not have explained it, and didn't seem like she much wanted to—even now—when she said, "Corey Dibiase said he thought the animal they delivered to the museum might have been a bear."

Louis would have expected more of a reaction from the giant. All Whitethunder did was shrug, nod his thanks to Lydia for filling his cup, and lean back again.

"That doesn't get a rise from you? I would have thought you'd be heartbroken to learn that the thing at the museum might not be your cousin."

"The Andean people, the Quechua, call bears ukuku, which means half-man."

"Okay?"

"In the end, it matters less what you call a thing, than what that thing actually is. All I know, is that it was my kin, my brother, I saw on that pedestal in the museum. I do not care if others deign to call it ukuku, or Sasquatch, or bear..."

An anxious little itch of anger pricked under Louis's skin. "Okay. Naming aside, I think Lydia and I might agree that if the DNA test comes back, proving that that thing is a bear, we'd both look at that as a disappointment, and at that thing in the museum as a fraud, regardless of how it makes you feel."

"The Cherokee thought bears were descendants of man," Clyde said. "I'm reminded of a story told to me many years ago concerning two clans who lived on either side of a river. They had warred for many years and then had many years more of uneasy peace. The leaders of both groups decided a marriage would be the best way to ensure the peace lasted. They planned a ceremony on the banks of the river, the daughter of one leader to marry a son of the other.

"Before the vows could be concluded, a great flood overtook the wedding party. The groom was caught up in it and carried away. He drifted on the river for days and days and when he finally got ashore, he was in a foreign land.

"Hungry after his trip, and cold, he realized that he did not know how to live on his own. In his clan, the men hunted in big parties, catching food for the whole community. The women would forage and make clothing for everyone. He was unaccustomed to doing things on his own, but he was wise enough to know that, if he was to survive, he would have to adapt, and quickly.

"At the riverside, he saw herons, swooping down to collect fish and he thought, I am as quick as a heron. And, so he waited at the riverside and when the fish would get close enough, he would try to grasp them. He was wrong, he was not as quick as a heron, but he soon grew to be.

"In the fields, he saw the small rodents grazing on berries. And he knew he could do that. He would lay out and graze all day.

"Soon, the fall came and he still had no clothing and no means of procuring any. Well, he thought, in the coldest part of the winters, the nighttime, I would bed down with my family and keep warm. So, I should treat the whole of winter as a chill nighttime. And he went and found a burrow and hunkered down and went to sleep.

"In the springtime, he was woken by the call of a woman's voice. He went out to meet her. It was his betrothed. But, seeing him, she knew they could no longer be together. He'd grown fur and gotten round and his nose and jaw had turned into a muzzle. She wept.

"Do not cry, love, he told her. We will always be one, even if we cannot be together and our families will always be one, no matter where they are. I am a bear now and I cannot die, so if you are ever in need—you or your family—call on me and I will come to you and give you my body for sustenance. That is the pledge I make to keep our families tied together. But do not be sad for my death. I am a bear and cannot perish."

"I'd hate to think about how many species of bear the human race has pushed to extinction."

"I don't think that was the point of the story, Louis," Lydia said after a sip of her tea.

THE EVENING MADE the nylon walls of Louis's tent glow purple, shimmering with brightness. It didn't last. The light sloughed away, and then it was the cold that kept him up, clinging to his cheeks and his nose and his chin. Pulling his knit hat over his face, Louis finally dropped off to sleep.

When he woke, it was in a panic. Someone was in the tent with him, hot breath on his face, something muzzy covering his eyes. He scrambled, kicking his legs and gasping.

"Relax, Louis, it's me," Lydia's whisper cut the silence. Reaching up and touching his face, Louis found the hat was still pulled over his chin. The warm puff of breath he'd felt had been his own. Pushing the hat up, he leaned forward. Lydia was barely in the tent—she'd undone the zipper enough to look in.

"What are you doing, Lydia? It's the middle of the night."

"Get up. We have work to do."

"It's... What time is it?"

"Keep your voice down, and hurry up." Then, she was gone, back outside the tent, zipping it closed behind herself. He could hear the weight of her body packing the snow as she stood.

He rubbed his face again, turned himself onto his side and wormed his way out of the sleeping bag.

His coat was cold and, standing out in the wilderness, it seemed like he'd left all his heat behind in the tent. He made fists, trying to get the feeling back in his fingers.

Lydia was already starting off into the trees.

"Hey," Louis whispered, "Why are we awake?"

She didn't answer. She paused and gestured to the ground. The campsite was run through with enormous tracks.

Peering down the short row of tents, Louis asked, "Clyde?"

Shaking her head, and continuing on, she said, "Gone."

With the snow cover—even with an overcast sky—it was easy to see where they were headed without the need of a flashlight. The trees were black around them, sighing and groaning in the breeze, crackling with the cold. The snowy ground seemed phosphorescent in the darkness, and the trail leading through it was clear enough to spot from twenty paces off. Leading between a spiny sprawl of evergreen boughs, the tracks disappeared into darkness, reappearing again, in a shallow glade on the other side.

Louis and Lydia paused, examining the distance for a moment. There was nothing remarkable in any direction. Little visible, at all.

Moving on again, in unison, they brokered the distance, following the trail back into tree cover.

Now and then Lydia would catch Louis's sleeve and make him pause and they'd stand still, listening. The woods were noisy with wintry sounds, the hiss of far off wind, the creak of frozen wood, but there was nothing remarkable to hear beyond that.

They moved on again. The path led them down a shallow incline and they traced along the edge of it, northward, before turning abruptly, following a long depression in the snow that might have been a snow-buried creek.

After following the path for a few dozen paces more, it disappeared into a nest of nighttime, where some heavy evergreen boughs sagged down. Lydia ducked to enter a little passageway into the nest and Louis ducked in behind her, so as not to shake free the snow weighing down the limbs. For a moment, everything appeared abysmal blackness and then chinks in the darkness took form, as the ground on the far side of the tree came into sight. After crossing through the nook beneath the tree,

Lydia stopped Louis again. Hunkered down, they both stared out across the illuminated forest floor to the blackness of the woods just beyond. The trail could barely be discerned, a deep blue stain bridging the distance.

"What do you…"

Louis's voice awoke a sudden excitement just ahead—the low boughs of a distant tree shaking, a slide of snow spilling off, hissing to the ground. A sudden pounding of footsteps railed away into the distance. Without the snow, the branch seemed to hide itself in darkness, suddenly invisible.

"Clyde," Louis muttered into his chest and lunged forward, freezing up when a hand fell on his shoulder, bracing him in place.

Louis turned to find Whitethunder standing in the darkness right beside him. The giant brought a finger slowly to his lips, before releasing Louis and emerging from the shadows where he'd been hidden, into the half light where Louis and Lydia crouched. Louis looked to Lydia. She looked as surprised as he felt.

"What the hell are you doing out here, Clyde?"

"Same as you. Tracking," he nodded his head in the direction the trail continued off, in the direction of the disturbed bough.

"Why didn't you wake us?"

"I thought it best to make as little noise as possible."

"Have you seen it?"

Clyde shook his head. "I paused here, because I thought the creature was alerted to me. Now, I am certain of it."

"Well," Louis said, "let's keep after it."

"We have gotten too far from camp." Clyde shook his head, whispering in his deep voice, "It is best we head back and pack up before following this trail any further."

"It's just ahead," Louis said. "Let's hurry, we can catch it."

Louis started forward, but was braced again by Whitethunder's enormous hand. Louis shrugged it off. "If we start rushing, it may hear us. If it runs again, we may have no hope of catching it."

Louis looked at Lydia. She nodded. "He's right. We have the trail. So long as it doesn't ford a river, we should be able to track it wherever it goes."

They turned back.

Louis couldn't help looking over his shoulder again and again, to the receding place where they'd almost caught their prize.

THEY PACKED QUICKLY and started out again.

By the time they'd returned to the spot they'd turned from, the sky was graying toward daylight.

Lydia motioned for them to hold up. Climbing out of the straps, she swung her rucksack in front of her. It landed with a whomp, tossing up a plume of snow.

A small folding shovel had been fixed to the side of the pack and she unstrapped it and assembled it and pulled a tape measure from a side pouch and pocketed it. Moving forward cautiously, she crouched sidelong to the nearest track and, with great care, removed the top layer of snow, exposing the print. It was almost a foot deep, but she only dug half that depth, before the basin of the print was exposed. There wasn't much to it—a flat depression, a slope of snow at the front where the forward motion of the foot had caused a landslide to run back into the long, wide divot.

Shuffling forward, she uncovered the next print in line, stood her shovel in the snow, and pulled the tape measure from her pocket. She measured the length of the closest print and then the width. She took a few photos, and then climbed back into her pack without a word.

After another twenty minutes of hiking, the day was lit in earnest, perfectly bright for them to find the end of the trail— dead-ended in an empty patch of forest, between two giant trees sprouting from the snow.

Lydia shook her head and looked at the ground and gave an exasperated cough.

"What now?" Louis asked.

Clyde was already moving forward again, saying, "Onward."

"Onward?" Lydia scoffed.

Clyde paused, turning back to her and answering as though he hadn't caught the tone of her voice. "Of course. The trail was headed in this direction, so this must be the direction we should continue moving."

Lydia stabbed her finger at the last, lonely footstep, sitting in the snow. "The trail ends, Clyde. I can see where it ends. I'm looking at it."

"To survive in the wilderness so long, undiscovered by man, one must imagine the being which we pursue has abilities of which we can only dream."

"Are you implying it flew?"

"I am making no implication at all. I am simply stating that the track was headed in this direction, and so that is the direction that makes the most sense for us to continue in," Clyde said. With that, he started off again.

Lydia turned away, shaking her head.

"What do you want to do?"

"Tracks don't just end, Louis."

"I know."

She let out a big puff of breath, cottony in the new day, and she started onward again, dropping into Clyde's trail.

IT WAS TWO HOURS further on before Clyde drew to an abrupt stop. Having lingered and drifted to the back of the pack, Louis broke into an awkward, loping gallop to catch up.

When he arrived beside the pair, Clyde and Lydia were both staring down. Before them, cutting through the trees, an uneven line of tracks was stamped deep into the snow, winding away in both directions, perpendicular to their own course. Again, Lydia dropped her pack and got out her shovel and tape measure. After excavating the track closest to her, she locked her tape measure and gently pressed it into the snow beside the print. Digging into her hip pocket, she came out with her phone, snapping a string of photos with the tape measure lined out in the long direction and then along the width. Exiting the camera app, she pulled up a GPS map and marked the location where they'd stopped. Looking in the direction the tracks seemed to originate from, she widened out the scope on the screen. "We're miles from anything," she said.

"Are they the same as the last ones?" Louis asked.

Lydia nodded, but didn't turn her attention from the trail. Resting her forearms on the tops of her thighs, she rocked back onto her heels and looked out into the forest ahead. "Eighteen and ten."

"Any clearer?" Louis asked.

She shook her head, staring into the distance. "Nope..."

Louis raised his gaze to see what she might be seeing. The forest stretched in every direction. Through the stripped tree-tops, he could make out the bulge of hills, white with snow, speckled with the black depth of the forest. He turned back to the tracks. "Could it be snowshoes?"

"Maybe." She turned her attention back down.

"They are not snowshoes," Whitethunder insisted in his monotone. "No. They are the tracks of the Sasquatch."

"You sound pretty confident," Louis said.

"Of course. Why would anyone snowshoe out here?"

Lydia raised her gaze over her shoulder to regard the man. "To trick us."

"That does not make sense. No one would have known we were coming this way."

Louis frowned at Clyde. "You knew..."

"Not beforehand. I have already explained to you that I am driven by a deep internal conviction. That is what has led us here—the calling of my ancestors."

Lydia was still wound around, watching Clyde through the corner of her eye. "Do you have anything to do with this trail, Clyde?"

"Of course! I have already told you, I am connected with this ancient clan. Our spirits are intertwined. When they move, I feel them moving inside me." He thumped his hand flat against his coat and it made a muffled thump.

Louis looked at Lydia. She watched Clyde a moment longer.

Turning to face the trail again, and pressing her hands to her thighs as she stood, she said, "We'll either find what we're looking for, or will have gone for a nice walk, I guess." She looked at Clyde, "Let's just not make this walk any longer than it need be, yes?"

"It will not be a walk. I am now convinced. I will find what I came here for." He started out, in the direction the trail wound.

The pair fell in behind him.

Lydia moved slowly, watching the branches for any sign of fur that might have gotten caught.

Louis fell to the rear of the pack again, and took a moment to cross the tracks, moving away from the path Clyde had blazed. He tried a few paces in stride with the mystery trail. If his legs had been a little longer, the gate would have been perfectly natural. He looked ahead to Clyde, plowing through the snow. The man was tall. The stride seemed to match.

THE FOREST OPENED ONTO a flood plain bordering a river. The snow there was thin, windswept, thinner and thinner the closer to the river the tracks led, until they disappeared altogether. The river hadn't frozen completely. A black vein of water ran down the center. The coldness of it seemed to hover in the air.

Pausing, Lydia gazed off, up river and then down. Snowy peaks crowded every direction.

Angling himself upstream, Clyde said, "The path was headed in this direction. There is no reason to think the Sasquatch would have turned abruptly."

Lydia looked at him a quiet moment, before returning her attention downstream. "There's also no reason to doubt it."

Clyde shrugged. "The day is coming to a close. We should make our camp here. In the morning, the way will become clear for us."

They set up their tents, away from the river.

Clyde went to the water to fill a collapsable water pouch that Lydia had stowed in her pack. While she worked at starting a fire, Louis stood off to the side, watching. A flicker of flame shimmied, mostly invisible in the dying daylight. A disproportionate plume of smoke rose from the wad of dried grass she was concentrating on. She puffed breath on the fire. The smoke started to thin and the flame grew brighter.

Louis said, "Do you think whatever made that trail actually has anything to do with the thing in the museum?"

After a moment, she shook her head dismally. Still crouching, with her forearms braced on her knees, she said, "I never had much faith in that thing in the museum in the first place."

Louis nodded, looking out over the snow-bleached landscape to Clyde, bent at the water's edge.

"How about you?"

"I wanna believe," Louis admitted.

"Good you can recognize that, I guess."

She took a handful of twigs from the pile she'd arranged beside her and placed them carefully over the flames, one at a time. The twigs crackled and caught.

Louis sat down quietly on his pack while Lydia continued working—loading on larger branches she'd sawed to size with the serrated edge of her camp shovel. After coaxing it up, she rocked back on her heels.

Speaking to the fire, she said, "I think there's a good possibility Clyde manufactured the cast he showed us in his shop. I think if he did that, there's more than a little chance he has something to do with the trails we keep running into."

Down at the river, Clyde was rising up, fixing the top on the five gallon pouch and turning to come back to camp.

"It's hard to figure how he could have gotten that far ahead of us."

Lydia nodded in agreement. "He certainly seems to know which way he wants us to go, though."

"Yes. Yes, he does."

Clyde was climbing the bank now, the snow growing deeper around his boots, a big, toothy smile pressed on his face.

"I figured you suspected the same."

Louis nodded and watched Clyde slog toward them, his boots sending up splashes of snow. "So, what does it say about us that we chose to follow him, anyway?"

"I don't believe you're following him, though, Louis. I believe you're following me."

"So, why are you following him?"

"I'm hoping I figure that out when we find it." She pursed her lips and shook her head. Clyde was almost there, laughing now, his laughter as loud as the roar of the river, clanging off the tree line. "Maybe it's just to find that final disappointment, so that I can let all of this go, knowing I turned every stone I found."

Clyde was among them now, dropping the water pouch at his feet. It collapsed to the side, listing loosely under its own gelatinous weight.

THE DAY DISAPPEARED, but beyond the narrow scope of light the fire cast, the world remained lit. Even with an overcast sky, the world remained lit. The snow brightened everything blue in every direction, and the river was black, and the tree trunks were black.

With the freeze dried meal Lydia had reconstituted consumed and gone, Clyde held on to his empty bowl as though he was making an offering to some fictive god, and his voice rang in the night, though it would have been impossible for an observer to know whether anyone was listening to him at all.

He said, "All this land was once the land of the Klallam." He nodded in every direction from his left shoulder to his right.

The wind blew and subsided. A lonely bellow. He said, "They were ravaged by the diseases of the White men even before the White men arrived. Blankets from ships infested with smallpox washed ashore. So, when the White men finally did arrive, the Klallam were already decimated. To the White men, it might have seemed the desolation was the very product of the Klallam's ways, and how could the Klallam insist anything contrary?

"The Klallam liked the White men's blankets, and did not know they had borne disease. They liked the blankets so much, they gave up breeding their wool dogs. The dogs turned to mutts and no longer produced wool.

"They liked the White men's potatoes. They grew quickly and cooked even quicker."

"—White men are the worst. Am I right, Clyde?" Louis announced loudly.

Lydia gave him a sharp look.

Clyde blinked slowly before continuing, "They liked the steel and the copper and the horses and the homes. They liked everything they saw and so, when the things that were theirs, the things that had given sustenance and identity to their ancestors were finally lost, it didn't seem like they had lost much of anything at all... Not at first.

"And, when the White man offered solutions, it seemed only natural to accept what was offered. The Klallam did not know that disease was the first real gift of these new neighbors; that all of the new man's gifts were diseases—felling trees by the acre, poisoning the air and the water, killing the traditions of the Klallam.

"The wild tribe, the Sasquatch, saw it all. They saw the great ships, drifting dead through the sea. They saw the blankets, washed ashore. They saw their brethren, the Klallam, sickened and dying. They saw the lies the new men spread. They saw his ways with nature. The wild tribe, the Sasquatch, retreated into the wilderness. Their way had always been the peaceful path and so it would continue, cloistered now, away from the world. Hiding for hundreds of years.

"They hid, but they continued to watch.

"It is my belief that they are ready to be known again. They will be protected, as their lands are now protected." He raised his hands slowly, but triumphantly, gesturing to all the land around them.

Louis shook his head. "White men. Always stealing everything, isn't that right, Clyde?"

"Louis," Lydia said, a note of warning in her voice.

"I mean, really, Clyde, the stealing never stopped, did it? You know, you see a redneck with a dreamcatcher hanging from the rearview of his pickup and a 'Make America Great Again' bumper sticker... Or a bunch of bros at a football game waving foam rubber tomahawks around. All it is is one privileged class taking everything from everyone else. It's the same as stealing land, in the end. In the end, nothing has changed. Don't you think, Clyde?"

"Louis..." Lydia said again.

Clyde shrugged and looked away. "It does not bother me: a White man with a dream catcher."

"No, I guess it wouldn't, would it..." Louis said.

"It is my belief that if White people spent more time imitating the Klallam, the world would be a better place, not a worse one."

"Kum by yah," Louis muttered.

Lydia shook her head and got abruptly to her feet, slipping away into the indistinct light by the tents.

Looking to the sky, Clyde said, "The history of humanity is a sad and bloody affair. But, it is just that: history. They say, those who don't study it, will be doomed to relive it, but it is equally true that those who study it too closely cannot help but live it as though it still possesses them..."

Louis cut Clyde off when Lydia passed back by the fire. "Where are you going?" He tilted his head to watch her pass.

Lydia did not pause, continuing toward the river, with a small box tucked under her arm. She raised the box up, over her shoulder and shook it and said, "What we came here to do. Work."

Louis struggled up from his seat, the snow crunching under him. "I'll come."

"Do what you want," she said, and she did not turn back and did not wait for him.

Hurrying to his snow shoes, he strapped them on and loped out after her, Clyde calling out behind them, "There is no point in looking tonight. That Sasquatch is not near. It would be a better use of your time, getting a good night's rest."

Neither Lydia, nor Louis responded.

THE NOISE OF THE RIVER gave motion to the blackness of the water, where it rested between blue shelves of ice. Lydia moved away from the noise, sinking into the darkness of the forest. Louis followed.

A hundred feet inside the tree line, Lydia stopped. Bringing her wireless speaker up in one hand, she looked down at her phone, sitting in her other, open palm. Tapping the illuminated play icon onscreen, a low, bellowing call issued from the speaker, echoing over the wilderness. In the silence afterward, she stood for a long moment, listening.

All Louis could hear was the quiet of the night, the distant hush of the river.

"Where'd the recording come from?" he asked.

Lydia gave him a quick, chastising look. From between her teeth, she whispered, "Tag along if you want, but please keep quiet. This isn't social hour."

"I'm not much good at social hour, anyhow..."

"Yeah. I noticed."

Louis sunk back and was silent. Lydia played the sound again, leaning forward, listening expectantly. The call rang off, through the trees. When Louis started forward again, snow crunching beneath him, Lydia seized his arm, drawing him to a stop. Releasing him, she told him in a tight whisper, "Don't move if I'm not moving. What did I say? Quiet. Quiet."

Louis nodded and waited and, when Lydia moved, he moved.

She made a path further away from the river, crossing into a stand of small, quaking aspens. It was a thin grove and, before long, they were back in the cover of the firs, where the land was darker. The snow was deep blue and the great width of the black tree trunks around them seemed to segment the land into unequal portions.

They walked until the hush of the river was replaced by the noise of the frozen trees standing in the frozen, still night. The wood popped and shrieked intermittently, and it made the night feel like a hostile crowd into which they'd wandered, welcomed with catcalls and jeers. And the silence between was a noise that seemed to exist solely inside Louis, like the sound hiding inside a shell; the sound of a vacancy inside himself.

They climbed a small rise.

At the peak, with the hill's roundness stretching away in every direction below them, Lydia raised the speaker and played the call again. Without the cushiony background of river noise, the call seemed somehow more insular: singular and sad. A lonely sound.

Lydia stood a long time, listening with the speaker held aloft. She listened longer than she might have needed and when she lowered the speaker, it was with a sigh. She turned to Louis. "Wilton. That's where the recording came from."

Louis nodded to the phone in her hand, somehow amazed that that sound, that storied sound which he'd grown up imagining, that call was here with him, his companion through the woods. It seemed to dispel any doubt about the creature they were stalking. "That's the sound?"

"It's been cleaned up digitally but, yes. That's the sound."

"I get the feeling you don't like talking about the Wilton Incident. It was such a landmark in your career."

"The biggest." Lydia exhaled. Her breath drifted like an apparition under the starlight. "It was also a long time ago."

She started forward again.

The hill bottomed out into a long lowland knotted with saplings. The land here seemed darker still; the little trees cluttering the underside of the high canopy were scraggy. Ahead, the land disappeared, the darkness in the distance composed of black, bobbing boughs, too scant and wispy to hold much snow.

Lydia raised the speaker and played the recording again. The noise echoed off into the distance while they both stood, motionless.

After a moment, Louis said, "I don't know what I did, but I didn't mean to upset you, Lydia."

She closed her eyes. She was quiet awhile before she said, "You know, if we had had a child, Michael and I, he could have been your age by now. We were too afraid, I guess. The world was hard enough. Bringing a child into it? I couldn't imagine.

"I miss him so much. All I have of him is a workshop full of garbage. A museum of bullshit that other people created so that the world would pay attention to them. It's all I have now. It feels inadequate. It feels like nothing at all."

Louis was silent. Lydia was silent.

She shook her head. She raised up the speaker and played the call out again. It echoed into the trees—somehow lonelier than before.

In the distance, a noise carried back, faintly, but there. Louis stood straighter. The breath caught in Lydia's mouth and, when she turned to look at Louis, her teeth and the whites of her eyes shone through the night. She nearly choked on the words, when she said, "Did you...?"

Louis nodded eagerly.

She tried the recording again.

They stood still, leaning into the hissing coldness to listen.

Nothing. Nothing but silence.

A tree popped. Another gave a big rusty yawn.

Lydia stayed still a moment longer and when she lowered the wireless speaker, it looked like it was the weight of a grave disappointment dragging it down. Even after her arm dropped, she stayed still awhile longer.

Staring into the distance, she asked, "You did hear it, didn't you?"

"Yes," Louis whispered. "I did hear it. Try it once more."

Lydia raised her hand and played the recording.

The cry pealed out into the trees. The silence following it seemed abysmal. They stood listening so long, the silence felt like the cold—something that might overtake them; something capable of destroying them.

"You really heard it?"

"Yes," Louis said. "I heard it."

"It wasn't just the wind? It wasn't just a tree settling?"

"No." He shook his head and said, "No. I don't think so. I did hear it."

She stayed still, staring into the distance, listening so hard that the record-player hiss of nothing-at-all seemed to become the very center of every sound. Standing so still, the coldness on Louis's cheeks settled into him. He shivered. Finally exhaling, and relieving herself her strained posture, Lydia dropped her arm.

Still, the woods were quiet.

There was no trail to follow and only a vague indication of the direction they should aim.

"Should we go back?"

Hope warming her voice, she whispered, "Let's go a little further."

"However far we go, we have to go back just as far," he reminded her gently.

She said, "I didn't ask you to come. You can go back, if you want. There's no chance you'll get lost if you follow our tracks."

Louis sighed. "A little further, then..."

They started forward. The way ahead was hard to navigate. Craggy brush, knotted together, limited the direction they could take. Lydia led the way, following a route of least resistance—a snaking maze-way through the brush.

Snow showered down on their shoulders from the shaken branches, as they advanced. Snow crept under Louis's collar, melting instantly, making his neck itch. His feet had felt like blocks since the day before, and even the difficulty of moving forward over the uneven terrain wouldn't warm them.

Emerging from the thicket, back into the high canopy of firs, Lydia came to an abrupt stop.

Before her, a line of long, wide tracks led off into the distance. She gave Louis a brief look, but neither of them spoke. Turning ahead again, Lydia stepped into the trail, hurrying along it cautiously.

The path sewed back and forth between the trees and, after only a few minutes of rushing along, a thin, orange light appeared in the distance.

Lydia drew to a stop. Only for a moment.

A little curse escaping her mouth seemed to launch her forward again, moving with a sudden, renewed ferocity. After another dozen paces, the shape of a lit window became clear, glowing dimly through the night, and Lydia was swearing with every step.

Behind her, Louis hurried to catch up, whispering, "Lydia. Lydia!" trying to stop her.

Maybe she didn't hear him.

She leaned forward, marching on, puffing and every breath seemed to have a curse buried in it.

Catching her by the arm, Louis managed to hold her up.

"What are you doing?" he whispered urgently.

"Don't you see what's happened, Louis? We're being toyed with. Those tracks are the same as the ones we were following earlier. They belong to whoever is in that cabin."

"You don't know that."

"Someone's in that cabin, Louis, and it's the same someone who's been leaving trails for us to follow."

Louis turned nervously toward the light.

It had vanished, the light extinguished. Now, there was nothing but the formless wilderness of nighttime in every direction. Louis gasped. "We need to get outta here. We need to get back to the camp…"

"What?"

"Come on," he tugged her sleeve, pulling her back along the path they'd already tread.

"Louis!"

"Keep your voice down." He looked back into the darkness behind them.

"What is it?"

"It's a meth lab, Lydia. It has to be. We need to go." He stopped pulling her. He didn't need to any longer.

They hurried back along the path they'd blazed.

"How do you know, Louis?" she asked, once they were on the other side of the thicket.

"Why the hell else would anyone be out here?"

Lydia didn't have an answer for that. She paused a moment and, taking her phone from her pocket, marked the spot on the GPS where she stood. Dumping the phone back into her pocket, she moved on again.

IN THE MORNING, when Louis emerged from his tent, he found Lydia already up, tending a pan set on a wispy fire. In the gray morning, the snow looked ashen and the bare aspens behind the campsite, like they'd been charred in a fire, but refused to ignite. The wind rose. Sails of snow poured from the ground into the air and the fragile flame of the campfire seemed to disappear. When the wind settled, the fire bloomed up again.

"Morning," Lydia muttered without looking his way.

Her tent had been broken down and packed away—seeming like it had vanished into nothingness. Her rucksack was leaned against a tree.

He sat across from her. "Been up long?"

She nodded absently toward the depression in the snow where her tent had laid and then to the fire, she said, "Little while. Don't know how you slept through my marching around. I didn't make any accommodations for you at all."

"That's nice," Louis looked around. "And Clyde?"

"I'd tell you if I knew." She turned her spoon in the pan. Even for its vanishing flames, the fire was too hot, an au gratin had formed along the edge of her pan; Lydia scraped it, folding it back into the uniform mush in the center.

Louis nodded, pressed his hands to his thighs and rose up, starting toward Clyde's pack, leaned against the stump of a rotted tree.

"I already looked," Lydia said.

Louis paused. "Nothing?"

"Nothing that would indicate he's been laying those tracks. But, we'll see what he has to say about his morning when he shows."

Louis sat again.

The pan was full of something brown, bubbling. The cold morning seemed to hoard any scent coming off it. Lydia doled some into a cup, stabbed a spoon into it and handed it to Louis. Even after a few bites, he remained unconvinced about whether or not it was chili. Other than a pervasive graininess, it seemed to have no texture at all; nothing in it resembling a bean or a scrap of meat. But, it was salty and hot and filling and it absorbed all of Louis's attention until, with a papery rasp of footsteps in the snow and a chatter of twigs, Clyde spilled from the brushes behind the campsite.

"Where..." Louis started to ask, but the words withered in his mouth.

Whitethunder was shirtless, his chest coated in fine, white hair. It made the dye job on his head seem even more absurd.

Louis leaned his elbow into his thigh. "Jesus, aren't you cold?"

"I am no colder than the day itself," Clyde said. It sounded like a boast. The man took a deep breath, closing his eyes, seeming to relish inviting the coldness deeper inside himself. Plopping down, crosslegged in the snow, he placed the bundle he'd been carrying in his lap.

Louis jerked back at the sight of it. "Jesus."

The man had a pair of rabbits, heads loose on their necks, the white fur around the mouth of one stained red.

"I caught them this morning. The All Seeing is with us—waiting to help us find the bounty hidden in winter's barrens. The All Seeing will lead us to my ancestors in the same way."

Louis stammered, not knowing where to begin with that bevy of bullshit. He said, "We have," he pointed to Lydia's pan in the fire, "whatever that is, to eat."

"It's chili," Lydia said.

"Here, I have brought fresh food," Clyde announced magnanimously. He jerked the rabbits up. They wriggled loosely on the tether with which he'd fixed them together.

"I'm not eating a rodent."

"Rabbits are not rodents," Clyde said.

"Like hell they're not."

"No, Louis, Clyde's right," Lydia put in. "Rabbits are Lagomorpha. They're a different species. Their teeth are different."

Clyde announced, "Also, their testes are in front of their penises."

"I don't care where their testes are," Louis said. "You could have them in your pocket and I wouldn't want to know."

Clyde ignored him. He said, "It is my intention to live from the land, whenever possible, for the remainder of this excursion. I believe it will bring me closer to the All Seeing and that, in turn, shall bring us all closer to that which we seek."

Louis turned to Lydia, hoping she'd intervene. When Clyde pulled a knife from the back of his belt, she finally broke her silence. "Why don't you save it for dinner, Clyde?"

He paused, his knife poised.

"We should try and get moving soon."

Clyde looked at Louis's tent. "Your friend has not yet packed up. By the time he has done so, my rabbit will be ready to enjoy." He shifted forward again, the knife tip dimpling the belly of his catch, only to pause again at Lydia's voice.

"It'll only take him a moment to break down, and we have food prepared already. We shouldn't let it go to waste."

The man lowered his knife and looked past Lydia's shoulder, considering it. Finally, he slid the knife back into the scabbard behind his back and said, "You are right, of course. In this cold, the rabbit will keep. Tonight I will prepare us a feast from the bounty of nature."

"I'm not eating a rodent," Louis said. "The time of day is irrelevant."

"It is not a rodent. Its testes are above its penis."

lutely nothing to make it more enticing to me."

Clyde shrugged. Lydia gave him the pan to eat out of. The man nodded, and through a mouth of mush said, "The All Seeing has been good to me. It will be a good day. That has already proven true."

"So, you were out hunting all morning?" Lydia asked.

In response, Clyde happily jigged his tether again. And so, a quiet fell over the campsite—all through breakfast, just the noise of tin cutlery on tin. All through breaking down the camp, just the crunch of feet in snow.

Finding a moment when Clyde was busy and Lydia nearby, Louis leaned aside and whispered, "Help me out. I haven't done a lot of camping. Is any of this normal?"

"He'll get cold and put his shirt on," she said.

That wasn't what Louis had been concerned about. Clyde's rabbits had been hung from a low branch nearby, drippings of blood bright in the snow below them. "Do you think it was him, answering your call last night?"

"I don't know, Louis. I don't have any more answers than you."

When Louis had his pack squared away, and had shrugged the straps onto his shoulders and tightened them down (the bag felt heavier this morning than it had the day before), he looked up to find himself standing between Lydia and Clyde, each of them drawing away in different directions, oblivious of the other.

When Louis announced, "Guys?" they both stopped, turning back to him; Clyde with his back to the river, Lydia at the head of the trail she'd blazed the night before. Looking back and forth between the pair, Louis said, "Maybe we should try and pick one common direction."

"The trail was leading up river. That is the direction in which we should continue," Clyde said.

Lydia said, "You mentioned yesterday that you thought the way would be clear in the morning, and so it is: Louis and I found another trail last night. I think it's time we find out where it ends."

"That's a bad idea, Lydia," Louis said. "I don't want to go back that way. Let's head up river. Clyde's been right so far." The last line hurt to let loose, but he did anyway.

"It's fine," she said, crossing back to him, pulling out her phone. After tinkering with the screen a moment, she aimed it at Louis. "See?"

On screen, her GPS map was up. It was hard to make out in the shock of snowy daylight. He shook his head.

"This," she said, pointing to a blip in the middle of the screen, "is where we were last night." She fiddled the screen again, drawing the view further out. "You see?"

Louis shook his head again, frowning. "No."

"There are no access roads anywhere, Louis. We're miles from anything."

"So?" Louis shrugged.

"A meth lab needs supplies. A meth lab needs to get meth out, to market. There's no road, Louis."

"What about a snowmobile?"

"Yeah, sure, if you want to leave trail anyone can follow. If you want to leave a trail that'll lead park rangers right to your door."

"Then, explain the light we saw," Louis leaned away from her.

"There's someone else out here. Someone who's leaving trails for us to follow. It's time we find out who it is." She looked to Clyde.

"I do not understand what you two are talking about," Clyde said, avoiding Lydia's gaze.

"We only have supplies left to get us through to the end of the day and then to get us back. So, before wandering further into the wilderness, we need to rule out that we're chasing the wrong thing," Lydia said. She dropped her phone back into her pocket and turned, starting away again.

"We have more supplies than that," Clyde called to her. "The All Seeing has opened her pantry to us."

Lydia didn't respond. She didn't turn. After casting Clyde a look, Louis fell in line behind the woman.

A moment later, Clyde fell in line as well, muttering loudly, "This is not the right way, this way you are taking us."

His voice was buried under the crunch of snow beneath them all.

THEY FOLLOWED THE TRAIL through the stand of aspens, where the noise of the river fell away. In the silence, Whitethunder found his voice again. "This is a waste of the day, trekking in this direction."

"How can you know that, Clyde?" Louis asked, only half-turning and not slowing at all.

"Because I know. I have told you, already. I have told you I have a deep, ancestral bond with the being we are pursuing. She did not come this way."

They climbed the hill and descended into the nest of hemlock saplings. Lydia found the trail they'd happened on in the night and didn't pause. Louis hopped outside her path and jogged up beside her, fighting through the deep, heavy snow. Panting with the effort, he said, "Are you sure about this, Lydia?"

She didn't answer. She kept moving.

Louis couldn't keep it up. Slowing, he fell back into the trail at her heels.

"She is not very pleasant this morning," Clyde observed.

Louis said nothing.

At the point where they'd turned back the night before, Lydia came to a stop, Clyde and Louis both abandoned the trail so they could come stand alongside her.

The cabin should have been in sight. Scanning the horizon, all Louis could see were tree trunks, black against the snow in every direction across the soft rise and fall of the pillowy ground. Louis turned to Lydia. She wasn't looking up, she stared at the ground. The trail they'd been following dead-ended—terminating in an open patch of snow, distant from every nearest tree by a dozen paces.

Turning to face Clyde, the softness of Lydia's voice belied its intensity, when she said, "Where is it?"

"I do not understand what you are asking me."

"The cabin. We found a cabin here last night. Where is it?"

Clyde looked at Louis. When he looked back in Lydia's direction he said, "I was not with you last night. How could I know such a thing?"

She spun again, launching herself into the virgin snow ahead. Louis hurried behind her. "It was probably just a reflection, Lydia."

"A reflection?"

"On some ice."

"A reflection of what? We didn't have our flashlights on," she said and marched away, in the vague direction of where they'd seen the window the night before. Louis thought she might be off by a couple degrees, but it didn't really matter—there was nothing to be seen in any direction but the breadth of wilderness, tree branches sagging with snow.

After another hundred yards, she stopped, her shoulders suddenly falling. "Damn it."

"Maybe we went in the wrong direction," Louis said.

"We followed our trail, Louis. How could we have gone in the wrong direction?"

"It has been speculated by some," Clyde offered in his sleepy, even tone, "that the Sasquatch are extra dimensional beings, able to slip in and out of this world at will. In fact, I remember you examining the very same possibility in *Recollections and Revelations from Wilton*."

Lydia turned slowly and gave the man a silent, sidelong look. She turned ahead again silent, still.

"Lydia?" Louis's voice was thin and cold in the cold, still air.

"What?"

"Lydia?" He repeated, more urgently.

She turned to find that he'd moved outside of the trail she'd made, wandering paces away. He'd come to a stop, staring down at the ground before his feet, to a plot three yards long that rose up at a perfect angle—a squat pyramid protruding from the easy undulation of the forest floor.

"What?" Now her voice was more insistent. She tromped through the snow, to his side, and when she landed beside him, she followed the angle of his view downward. There, on that flat incline, a perfect grid was mounded with snow, twelve perfectly regular, rectangular holes snugged up together. The basin of the holes was filled with soft powder.

Raising his snow shoe, Louis stomped on the incline. The snow on the grid spilled off. Cleared, it was obvious they were looking into a window in a wall that had long since fallen, the glass long since shattered and scattered away.

Lydia shook her head and wound around, gazing out, across the landscape. "It's just an abandoned cabin, that's all." She gestured to the empty wilderness around them. "There're are a ton of them out here, from before this land being protected."

"This is exactly where we saw that window last night. Exactly."

"So?" She shook her head. "What are you getting at?"

Whitethunder answered for him. "It is possible our friend is a visitor from the far past, or a distant future, and what you two saw last night was a glimpse into another time."

The man's naked shoulders steamed in the day.

Lydia shook her head more violently and started off again, following her own path back toward where they'd come from. Slowing, coming around Whitethunder, she said, "What we're looking for is flesh and blood—a mammal, a primate, Mr. Whitethunder. We are looking for something that can be examined and catalogued. We're not chasing fairytales." Louder, to Louis, it seemed, she announced, "What we saw last night was clearly some sort of optical illusion. A reflection of some unseen light source, perhaps our own fire. Whatever left that trail is unrelated. Whoever left it must have doubled back in his tracks. We'll follow the trail back, to wherever it came from."

She set out again, taking the trail back toward the brush.

They passed through clear, wide forest, over shallow hills and down a steep incline, where the noise of the river became evident again. There, again, coming up against a wall of scrag brush, the path terminated.

Lydia yanked off her cap and dashed it against her thigh. She combed back her hair—damp with sweat and matted—taking a deep breath, and resuming her composure. For a long, quiet minute, she examined the way ahead with a slow, analytic gaze.

"There," she finally announced, pointing forward. "There."

Louis came up beside her. "Where?"

"You see that disturbance?"

Ahead, beyond the scrub, on a flood plain beside the river, the snow was mussed, a big patch of it cratered like a still frame of rough sea. Tracks led away in several directions.

"What are you saying?"

"Well," Lydia said, "It must have jumped."

Louis frowned and was silent a moment. Silent, until he said, "I don't know, Lydia... That's a long way."

"What other explanation is there, Louis?"

Whitethunder was quiet behind them.

"Still," Lydia said. "This place does seem familiar." She took a breath and gazed up at the tree tops.

"Yeah. It's a dead end," Louis muttered, "We've been finding a lot of those."

Behind them, Whitethunder said, "It is familiar because it is our campsite. Those disturbances are our footprints and the prints left by our tents."

Lydia let out a groan that sounded like it might be the beginning of tears, but then she shook her head and cleared her throat and turned, marching past the two men once more.

"He's right. Whoever made the trail must have slipped off somewhere along the way."

She followed the trail back slowly, keeping her eye to the ground, all the way to the fallen wall Louis had found.

Slowly inching forward, watching the ground on either side of the trail, Lydia made her way back along the path through the brush. Louis lagged back. He didn't bother looking at the ground, he gazed out at the landscape around them and ate meal bars as tough to chew as paperbacks.

By the time they'd returned to the river, the cloud cover had grown dark and ominous. A constant, cold wind had started blustering. Clyde didn't pause to consult, he simply struck out in the direction he'd been headed that morning. Louis hooked his thumbs in the straps of his backpack and turned to Lydia.

"How long should we indulge this?"

Lydia shrugged. Starting off, after the giant, she said, "Until he gets us to whatever it is he wants us to see, or the sun goes down, I guess. Whichever's first. Tomorrow, we'll have to head back, regardless of the outcome."

CLYDE HAD TIED THE rabbits to his rucksack with a length of rawhide. They swung like a metronome, synched to the pace of his footsteps, leaving a bloody arc across the leather. There was no choice but for the pair behind him to watch the gross display, as Clyde was now their leader.

Ahead, the height of mountains had been decapitated by a froth of cloud. The wind had picked up. The trees swayed. Wisps of snow shuddered about, picked from the branches and pushed by the wind and Louis didn't understand how Clyde took the cold without a shirt. Even with his gloves on, Louis had to make fists, squeezing this hands closed tight to fight off the numbing cold. The pads of his feet felt like stones lodged in the innersoles of his boots.

Turning a bend, the river narrowed and seemed enraged; the water black and roiling. The banks alongside it all but disappeared. There, Clyde redirected their course into the cedars at the water's edge. The boughs were weighted with snow and when Clyde pushed through they unleashed their bounty, snow sizzling through the needles and dousing his shoulders. Free of the weight, the branches rose gracefully from Clyde's path, like sentinels parting spears to offer entry.

Brushing the snow from his shoulders with the back of his hand, Clyde gave no indication that that powder was chilly in the least.

Pausing between two cedars, when the man stopped suddenly, Lydia broke into a sprint to come along his side. She had to push her way into the boughs to get room beside him. Nestling his way into the branches on Clyde's other shoulder, Louis emerged to see what had brought them all together.

A trail of prints traveled up from the river, cutting out into the wilderness away from them.

"Oh. Well," Clyde said, sinking back, "it would seem we have found our trail again."

"Perhaps," Lydia said, and she retreated from the tree and slung her backpack off her shoulders and let it down into the snow.

Louis turned to look at Clyde.

The man continued staring at the ground and would not return Louis's gaze. Louis couldn't keep it up long; a moment later Lydia was behind them, saying, "Move aside, fellas; some of us have work to do."

Louis pushed his way through the boughs, hopping over the tracks and finding a position in the narrow clearing between the trees where he could watch her work.

Clyde moved aside for her.

Emerging from the boughs, she frowned at the trail and slowly turned her scowl up to Louis. "In the future, please don't cross over a track until I've had time to examine it."

Louis looked down the trail and gestured broadly. "Doesn't seem like you have any shortage to investigate."

She looked at him steely. "Don't cross a track, Louis, before I've done my work."

"Yes. Sorry."

She worked, digging out the tracks, measuring and taking photos and when she was done, the tight gap between the trees was fairly trampled and she stood straight, still frowning at what they'd found.

"Well?" Louis asked.

She nodded. "They're the same. The dimensions are the same. The gate is the same. The depth is the same. But, again, very little detail." She gazed out into the forest ahead. "Impossible to tell if they're snowshoe tracks or foot prints."

Louis looked back and forth between the pair.

Clyde seemed to have no expression at all. Lydia's frown didn't abate. She'd turned to Clyde, staring for a long, steely moment before turning, and walking back toward the river. Pushing the boughs there aside, she peered out at the undulating, black water. Louis came up beside her.

She said, "It doesn't seem right."

She shook her head. Turning, she found a broken branch caught in the boughs of a nearby tree. Tearing it out of its place, she took a moment to strip some of the tertiary sticks from its length. Back at the water's edge, she plunged it into the water pouring past. When she pulled it out again, the depth of the river was marked on the stick, almost four feet, right beside the bank. The water was quick and rippled.

She shook her head. Turning to Clyde, she said, "It doesn't make sense. That's deep. Why would any animal not just come up on shore? Why would it have waded out through that icy water to this point before coming up?"

"Why ask me?"

Lydia shrugged. "Well, you purport to have a deep connection with this creature, yes?"

Clyde pondered it silently for a moment. "Perhaps it was fishing."

"At this time of year? There're no salmon."

"Perhaps it was cleaning itself. The Klallam were known to wash daily, regardless of the weather or time of year."

She turned to face him. "Here? With this current?"

Clyde shrugged. "Perhaps it is a different Sasquatch; perhaps it needed to cross the river and chose this point. Or, perhaps it is the same Sasquatch and it realized that we were following it and it was doing its best to throw us off. There is no way of knowing. What is certain, is that it came through this way and that if we follow the track, we are sure to find it. Once we have found it, perhaps we will discover why it acts the way it acts."

"Yes. Perhaps," Lydia echoed him and turned and propped her measuring stick against the boughs of the closest cedar and left it there. Crossing back between the men, she retrieved her backpack, where she'd left it in the snow, and hoisted it back on.

Louis turned to Clyde. "And you, Chief Where's-Your-Shirt?"

"Do not call me that."

"...Well, why do you look so damned disappointed? Isn't this exactly what you thought we'd find?"

"I am not interested in finding trail. I am not interested in finding sign. I have found that before. It is my intention to find the Sasquatch; to see her myself; to make contact with her. We have lost half a day, heading in the wrong direction. There is little to celebrate in that."

WITH LYDIA PREPARED, they started off again, following the trail away from the river. It wove between the trees and must have been fresh from the prior day, or maybe that morning—the snow was cleared from the low boughs, the prints were precise.

The cedars thinned away and they came through a stand of red alder and then back into the darkness beneath the towering Douglas Firs. The trail led to the base of a sheer cliff and ran along side it for a hundred paces before ending abruptly.

Lydia's head jerked like she'd been caught in a car wreck. Staring straight ahead, she pulled off her hat, pinching her temples with her free hand. She did not move and, even after Louis and Clyde had made an unorganized search of the immediate area, she still hadn't budged from her spot. Eyes closed, her long, gray lashes gleamed wetly.

When Louis and Clyde returned to her, she opened her eyes and they were dry but crazed looking. "Someone laid this trail, backtracked, and ducked away into the woods. This is the same thing we've already found—the same damn trick." Her attention, the rage in her eyes settled on Clyde.

Surveying the distance, Clyde's head rotated away from her so slowly, it was as though he were tracking a tortoise. Lydia kept staring at him as his gaze settled on the imposing face of stone beside them. Just as slowly, he raised his hand and pointed his finger up at the shelf, high, high above. Lydia swung her head up viciously.

Huffing, she turned back to Clyde. "You're joking."

"A strong climbing ability would be useful in avoiding detection. Such skills may account for the illusiveness of the Sasquatch."

Lydia shook her head. "No animal could climb that face, Clyde."

"A skilled free climber could find his way up."

"Yes, maybe. We're not tracking a free climber, though, are we?"

"The creatures of the forest of are often innately capable of what human beings might consider impossible. The bird can fly, but until a hundred years ago, most humans considered such a feat beyond the scope of human capacity."

"A Bigfoot did not climb that face, Clyde."

Clyde nodded knowingly up to the heights above. "I believe I could climb that face, if I had a mind to. The All Seeing would guide my hands and my feet along the best route and I would find my way. The creatures of the forest are closer to the All Seeing than we are. It makes the improbable everyday."

Lydia shook her head and looked to the ground. After a fevered breath she turned, starting back along the way they'd come, keeping wide of the trail they'd already laid.

"Where are you going?" Louis called.

She soldiered forward without pause. "Whoever made that trail, backtracked and took off. I'm gonna find which way he went."

Louis looked at Clyde. The man was still staring up, as though trying to discern the easiest route along the face. Shrugging, Louis turned to follow Lydia, keeping to the opposite side of the trail from her.

The grove of tall Douglas Firs kept the forest floor open, so that every undulating direction could be seen around them. Tracks should have been easy to spot. Even so, Louis and Lydia kept wide from the trail, crossing around the backsides of the nearest trunks, as wide as five big men in a clutch. No trail led away.

They passed back through the patch of alders, slim trunks white against the whiteness of the snow, the sky exposed, heavy above them, shedding snow more steadily now. Even here, it seemed as though an unseen escape route would have been impossible.

They found no trail.

Reconvening before entering back into the cedars along the river's edge, Louis surveyed the snarl of branches and shook his head. "We're talking about a long way to back track, here, Lydia. A long way."

She looked at him. "What's more likely, Louis: someone climbing that face, or taking the time to backtrack?"

Louis chewed his lips and stared forward into the dark grove of cedars. He nodded silently, and they broke apart, Lydia taking the wide right along the route and Louis taking the left.

Getting through the boughs was an effort. The trail they'd followed had clearly led through the way of least resistance, and beyond it the heavy branches of the cedars barred the way in every direction. Louis pushed through, snow raining down on him the whole time, his snowshoes snared by low branches. He was panting and damp by the time he came out the other side and met Lydia again, by the bank of the river. There, the wind iced the perspiration on his face.

She asked, "Anything?"

Louis shrugged. "It's hard to see in there, Lydia. Snow was dropping everywhere."

"So that's it, I'd say. They must have come though that way—we just failed to find the trail."

He shrugged again and turned back, facing the wilderness they'd just navigated twice. "Maybe. Where do you think Clyde went off to?"

Instead of answering him, she shouted into the distance, "Clyde!"

Her voice died, swallowed by the soft arms of the cedars, swallowed by the noise of the river and the cold air, and the growing hiss of falling snow. A breath later, a vague hoot returned—Clyde's voice, far off.

Louis snorted. "You think he's trying to climb that cliff?"

Lydia stretched her neck and sighed to the heavens. Her breath piped out like exhaust from a mill stack. "He's probably broken his neck by now."

"Should we head back and get him?"

She puckered her mouth and shook her head. "Let's head upstream and see if we can't find the way our trickster went. Clyde can follow our path once he gets tired, trying the impossible."

THE RIVER GREW NARROWER, the sound of water rising in a tumult and the air growing colder with dampness. The snow was coming faster now, increasing in pace as the noise of the river grew and once they'd rounded a bend, they found a tall waterfall, tossing water out from under a roof of ice and sending a constant breath of mist across the river basin. Mist had frozen to the tree trunks facing the river, covering them in a pale, gleaming armor. The pair paused and took a moment to look around, and as Louis's gaze reached the top of the waterfall, he was suddenly struck still. Still staring upward, he tugged the sleeve of Lydia's jacket, like a child. She looked at him before following the path of his stare, toward the low sky.

Standing to the side of the falls, Clyde's pale, naked torso could be seen, just over the wall of rock. He waved an arm ecstatically. When Louis finally got his senses back, he cupped his hands around his mouth and shouted upward, "How the hell did you get up there?"

Clyde shouted back. His words were buried in the noise of the falls.

Louis shouted a second time. Now, Clyde's response was to point down to the river basin. There, shy of the falls, a toppled tree, sheered of its branches, bridged the river banks. On the far side, a crop of fallen rock made a chaotic staircase up to the top.

The tree trunk was covered in a thick, milky enamel of ice.

Lydia doffed her rucksack and set it in the snow and took off her snowshoes and tied them to the pack and had Louis do the same with his.

With one end of a length of rope belted around her waist, she straddled the trunk and scooted across, hugging the width with her legs. Louis held the other end of the rope, feeding her slack as she went.

Once she'd crossed, under her instruction, Louis tied his end to a sturdy looking tree and, before making his own crossing, fixed the packs to the line with carabiners and tied a second rope to them—a second rope, which he trailed behind him as he crossed the cedar, holding tight to the line Lydia had run.

The water churned, cold and black beneath him and he tried not to look down and tried not to think about how slick the trunk was between his thighs.

When he'd finally crossed, they pulled the packs to them and threw them on. Even in such a short time, the fabric had grown a thin skin of ice which flecked away as they shouldered their way into the straps.

Buckling crampons onto their boots, they climbed the icy ladder of rock. When they reached the top after a long, exhausting scramble, the fluttering snow had turned the gray day indistinct, and Clyde stood waiting for them, naked from head to toe, save his boots and the snowshoes beneath them.

Louis bent in half, a sudden convulsion of laughter robbing him of his breath.

"Jesus Christ." Lydia covered her mouth. "You need to put your clothes on, Clyde. You're going to catch hypothermia."

"If I become cold, I will put my clothes back on. But, you do not need to worry. My people were made for this weather."

'Swedes,' Louis thought caustically, his laughter wilting.

The man's poor penis, poking from a white-gray bush of seventies porn-star proportions, looked like a worm that had been dried out on August concrete; shrunken, brittle and red. His skin was chapped pink all over.

Lydia, apparently, could think of nothing more to say. She shook her head and when Clyde started away, she fell in behind him, her head still shaking.

Beyond the head of the falls, the river widened out again and grew steadier, more peaceful. Snow fell on the black water and vanished. Any quiet gained by the growing distance from the falls was stamped out by an increasingly furious wind. Cold pins of snow slashed through the air, stinging Lydia's face and Louis's face and biting Clyde Whitethunder head to ankle. The man's skin grew pinker and pinker, but he did not shudder, and he did not complain.

THEY CONTINUED ON, the storm worsening. The visibility before them grayed deeper and deeper, closing in around them until, when Louis lifted his head from the tracks he was stepping into, all he could see was Lydia's black garb and Clyde's pink ass, his dun colored back pack and his black, whipping hair, appearing and disappearing between veils of gray snow.

The wind fought them, and every step became more difficult. Finally, the gusts stopped them, bringing them all together. Hollering over the gale, Lydia said, "We can't keep going like this! We need to get into the forest and make camp!"

"It is not necessary, the All Seeing has shown me: there is refuge for us ahead! We are almost there!"

Shaking her head in a fit, Lydia said, "Clyde, it would be a lot easier to take you seriously, if you weren't naked right now!"

"I am in my natural state! Please, a little further! The All Seeing guides me!"

Lydia shook her head and turned away from the river. Passing Louis, she said, "Do what you want. I'm going to make shelter."

Louis looked at Clyde, but only for a moment before turning and following Lydia into the cover of the trees.

Inside the canopy, things weren't any better. Hidden by the blizzard, the trees above Louis and Lydia tossed violently, shrieking and popping.

Finding a spot that seemed level and protected, Lydia unrolled her tent and had Louis hold it while she searched her bag for stakes. After pinning a corner into the snow, she handed a stake off to Louis. The moment he let go of the corner he'd been holding, juggling a stake in the palms of his gloves, the tent pulled from the ground, tumbling across the snow, snagged after twenty paces around the trunk of a tree.

The snow billowed for a moment. The tree disappeared. When it shuddered back into sight again, the tent was gone altogether.

Lydia dove for Louis's pack, tearing his tent free. Unfurled, the wind tugged at it and it seemed like Lydia might be next to go airborne. Louis grabbed ahold, too. Together, they wrestled the whipping fabric down. Once the corners were staked Lydia tried to feed the center pole into the back rib, but the tent filled with air and blew off into the distance, fading into the gray instantly.

Louis stared after it, his eyes wide but soaking up nothing but grayness.

Lydia wasted no time. Throwing her rucksack back on her shoulders, she grabbed Louis by his collar, screeching over the wind, "Get your bag! Follow me!"

Louis did as he was told, following Lydia's vague, shifting silhouette around the backside of a huge tree trunk. There, they dropped down, huddling together as the snow mounded up in windrows on either side of them. The world before them was gray and grainy and ever-darkening—seeming to disappear before their eyes, eaten whole by snow. Snow piled in Louis's lap. He stared forward.

He was going to die here, cowering in the cold—he was suddenly certain—the world gone gray and apocalyptic around him. Forget the massive coronary, he would die like this: swallowed by a gray waste of wilderness. And why was he even here? *Why?*

He should be with Maria now, half a knot of loving arms. He shouldn't ever have left her. He should have finished that damned book. This trip had changed nothing. Nothing, except he would be shuffled off without a final "I love you," to cherish.

He couldn't bring her voice to mind. All he could hear was the screaming wind, and it was all he could feel—other than his own sinking heart. All he could see was the thickening gray, closing in over him... dying... drifting into death...

"Hey!" Lydia's voice broke the might of the wind. Her hand clawed his thigh.

Louis turned to her.

Her face was a pucker of windblown agony, her eyes narrowed so tight they were only slashes of gray eyelash buried in her face. She reached up and grabbed his cheeks with her ice-matted gloves, pulling his face close. "Keep it together! We're going to get through this! Together!"

He nodded and turned away.

The gray before them bulged and bellowed, the snow whipping past, parallel with the ground. Icy flecks stung his chin and cheeks and the backs of his wrists where his gloves had come away from the sleeves of his jacket.

He would keep it together. He had to... It was his only hope of ever seeing Maria again.

Still, that need to remain calm twisted itself into an impossible dictate, a shrill, bastard mantra, the moment he turned forward, facing gray-death again. Before him, stuttering closer through the ashen veil, a dark figure began to coalesce.

It was his grandfather there, coming to damn him.

No. It was the Sasquatch, lumbering through a land it alone was king of—the last remnant of a wild that could not be tamed by a civilization whose only concern was the monetization of everything.

No.

No. It was not that, either.

It was Clyde, stomping naked through the snow, reaching down and grabbing Louis by the jacket—hauling him up.

Louis could no longer stand. He could no longer breathe. It was like the snow was stuffing full his mouth. He gasped, staggered and started to fall.

Clyde crawled under his arm, lifting Louis along. He turned to Lydia, "Come along! I have found a cabin where we can wait out this weather!"

"How far is it?!"

"It is not far," Whitethunder yelled back at her. He helped Louis along, and Louis was in such a deep panic, he barely noticed that the man's shoulders his own arm rested over was naked; barely noticed that the man's hip rubbing against his was naked.

Louis barely noticed anything at all until the darkness ahead stared to grow.

At first, Louis thought it was only the storm further darkening the world, until they were close enough so he could see the weathered gray boards of a doorway and Louis was finally certain where they were: a meth lab; the domain of the wintry undead, opening wide to consume him—gray and weathered in a withered, gray land. Louis tried to fight, to get away, but in the end, he was done. His legs buckled beneath him and his mind went black as he was submerged in the darkness beyond the door.

LOUIS'S PANIC ATTACK had subsided, but he remained quiet, staring into the darkness of rotten boards above him.

Clyde calling the place a cabin had been a dubious generosity. The backend had been crushed by a felled tree in some distant past. The chimney and the front wall had lasted—somehow—and held the sunken roof up so the place was more lean-to than anything. Flurries of snow drifted in through the gaps in the wall boards. Until the wind died, it seemed like the whole place might just go airborne around them.

But the wind did die. The snow stopped sputtering in. And, after that, the wood could be heard, popping and sizzling in the fireplace. And everything else seemed terminally quiet.

Crouched beside the fire, Clyde tended to the rabbits he'd caught, the carcasses smoldering over the flames, the meat charring and crackling. Clyde's drowsy voice filled the cabin.

"The world was once in perfect harmony, a balance maintained by all of the powerful spirits. The elk and deer and buffalo feasted on endless banquets of prairie. And, when there were too many, and not enough food, the wolves would come through. Following the wolves, many others came forth to share the bounty. The bears would take their share and the ravens and crows would have what remained. The world was in balance. Then, it all changed.

"Man came forward and divided the natural order. Where wolves would share with the bears, men would not.

"The ravens and crows faired better.

"With use of the air, they could come and help themselves to men's things. And though he did not like it, though he did not share in the way the wolves would, man was given no choice in the matter. The black birds had always taken what they would like, and never did ask.

"The bears tried too, but when they failed at securing some of the men's food, they quickly discovered that they would become a part of the meal. The great grizzly, the king of the bears, assembled his council to discuss the matter. It is not fair, they all agreed. Something must be done—they agreed again, but could come to no consensus about what. The meeting adjourned without resolution. The grizzly, being the wisest of all and seeing a paucity of original thought on the matter, decided to consult outside his own troupe.

"In the deep, deep forest, he found a murder of crows. They barked at him and laughed at him and spoke about him in their own tongue, as if he were not there, when he asked for help. His pride wounded, the grizzly chased them off, before going on his way.

"Further along, he found a group of ravens and asked them, 'What shall the bears do to correct the upset order?' In the manner of ravens, they sat, perched high in the trees with their backs to him, and would not answer.

"Soon, he had gone further than any of his kind had ever gone, to where the rivers left the land, the very edge of the earth. There, he saw something miraculous. On the ocean was a boat. He noticed that, as the men aboard threw out their chum and dragged their nets, for every succulent gob of rotten meat that landed in the water, another would find its way into the cawing mouth of a hovering seagull. The bear watched this all day. When the boat came in, he happened to find a gull who didn't seem to mind speaking with him.

"'Tell, friend, how do you have such easy ways with men that they feed you? How have you managed to turn them from their own greed?' The gull laughed—gulls are always laughing. 'They do not share with us willingly, friend. Men have only greed and so the only way to coexist is to be clever.' The bear did not understand. 'Perhaps it would be best if I showed you,' said the gull. Picking up a clam from the sea side, the gull placed it before the bear. 'Now,' said the gull, 'take it as quick as you can.' The bear nodded and ambled forward, but before he could get the clam, the seagull had swooped in and devoured it whole. 'Perhaps, we should try again,' the gull suggested. They tried again. Again, the gull was quicker, seizing the prize and taking it down.

"They tried again and again until the day was done—the gull was so full he could not move and the bear was so hungry he couldn't do much more than that himself.

"Belching with satisfaction, the bird told him, 'You are, perhaps, too old to learn new ways. If you give me a child, now, I think I should be able to teach him.'

"And so it was arranged. The bear brought a cub to the seagull and left it there, agreeing to come back in three years time to see what progress had been made.

"Time passed and the bear returned. He hardly recognized his offspring, when he saw it, but the little bear had learned the clever ways of the seagull so well, that he wore a dark mask around his eyes that was befitting a sneak. He was small, too, and quick and had clever hands.

"'Now, the raccoon is the king of the bears,' the seagull announced and laughed—gulls are always laughing.

"Too small to truly be a king, the grizzly thought. But, he supposed that this new bear was royal, in its own way."

Clyde fell silent. In the sudden absence of his voice, it was the smell of rabbit meat that overcame the cabin and Louis's stomach clutched with hunger. It was so enticing, after a day of brown mush for breakfast and meal bars for lunch, and the exhaustion of the storm and his panic, that he knew he would not be able to resist it, despite his earlier insistence. It was so enticing, Louis couldn't even find the will to argue Clyde's ludicrous story—Even if raccoons were related to bears (which seemed implausible), there was no reason that any folklore should make that claim. Besides, raccoons were almost certainly rodents—they behaved exactly as rodents did and looked like rodents, too...

Completely naked now, without his boots or snowshoes, Clyde worked by the light of the fire with his knife, dividing the rabbit meat and when that was done, he rose up, crossing to a crookedly hanging cabinet, clinging desperately to the bowing wall beside the chimney. Opening the door, Clyde pulled out a stack of enameled tin plates. Back at the fire, he plated the meat, delivering a plate to Lydia and then one to Louis. Louis sat up to take it, and thank the man. Clyde nodded and returned to sit with his back before the fire, a plate of his own secured in his lap.

Louis dug right into the meat, slick with grease and rich, but Lydia didn't touch hers. Instead she sat silently, watching Clyde move about the cabin and, now, watching him as he returned to his place in front of the fire to sit and eat.

"Clyde?"

The man paused chewing to raise his head and look at Lydia. With the fire at his back, his face was all in shadow.

"How did you know there were plates in that cupboard?"

Clyde lifted his chin, an acknowledgment that he'd heard the question. Beyond that, he gave no response. Now, Louis had given up spooning food into his mouth, as well. He swallowed the bite he'd already taken and watched Clyde.

"You said the All-seeing led you here. Did the All-seeing lead you to those plates?"

"I have been here before," Clyde said. "In past treks, searching for the Sasquatch, I have bedded in this cabin."

"So, it wasn't the All-seeing that led you here. Why did you lie about that?"

"There is no lie. Is it not possible to be led somewhere one has previously been?"

"Clyde, you intentionally misled us. You know you did."

The man was silent, until he said, "Why should I have wasted our time doing something like that?"

"You tell me," she said.

But, he did not. He sighed. He bowed his head and returned to eating.

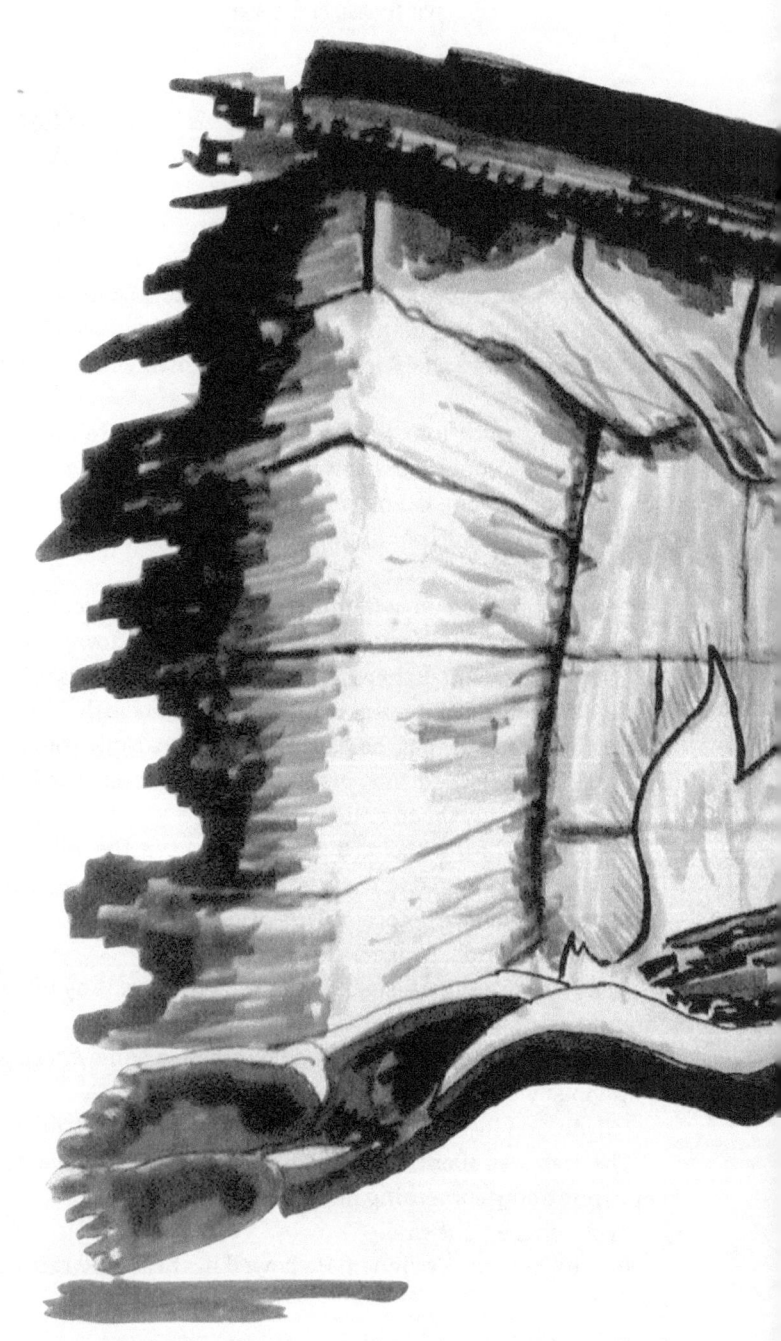

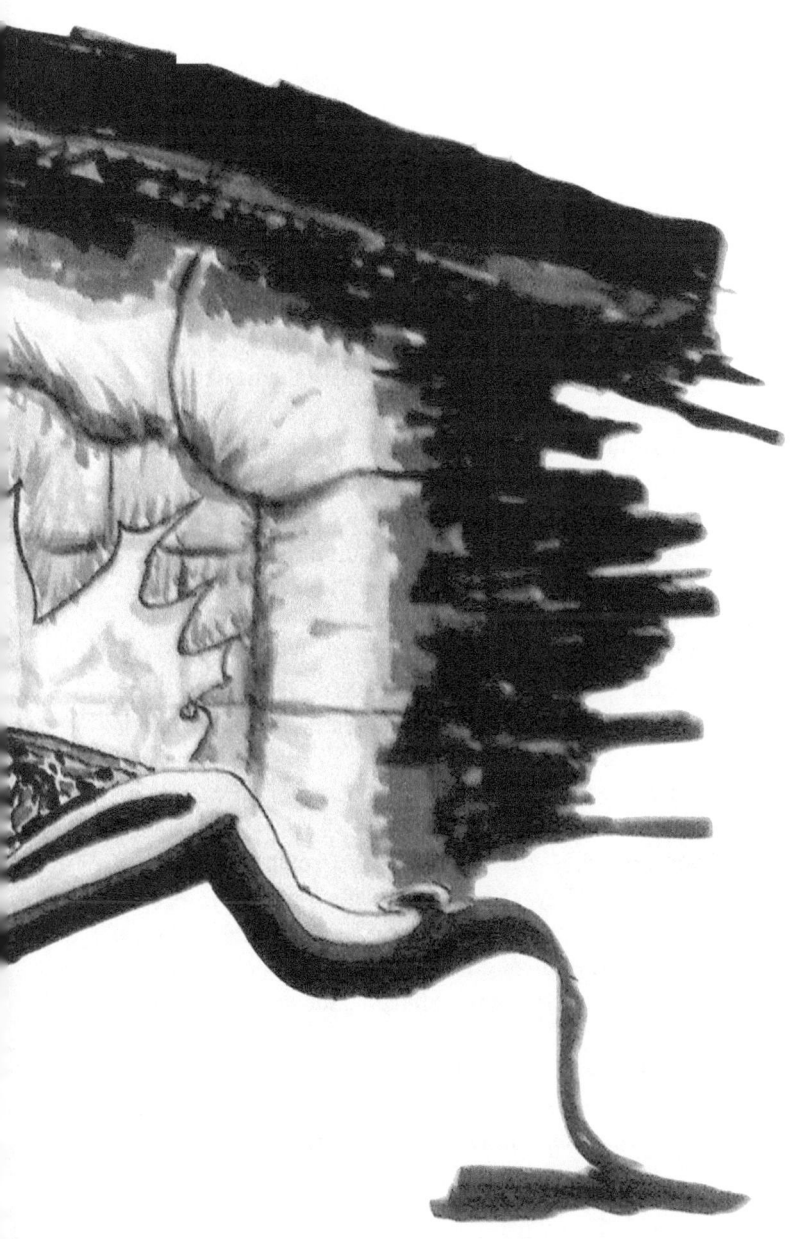

WHEN THE SOUND OF Lydia's Bigfoot call broke through the night, Louis opened his eyes and turned away from the wall. The fire was still writhing in the crooked mouth of the fireplace, and Clyde was curled before it, faced away, his nakedness candescent in the darkness. Squirming out of his sleeping bag, Louis gathered up his snowshoes, and snuck out the door.

Outside, he buckled his snowshoes on and turned to the tracks in the snow. With fresh powder piled over everything, it was clear which trail led to Lydia. And, when the noise of the call cut through the night again, he followed the tracks away from the river, into the darkness between the trees.

Lydia had not gotten far. Louis found her in a wide clearing, standing still and listening. The sky was clear, the landscape glowing with moonlight. Hearing Louis close in, Lydia turned briefly. Facing back ahead without a word, the pale ghost of her breath glowed in the night air for a moment, before it vanished.

"Mind if I join you?"

"No, I don't mind," Lydia said and started away.

Louis followed. They crossed the clearing and entered a grove of aspens. The leaves were gone, of course. The branches set rivers of blackness through the galaxies above, and again through the snow beneath them—sharp shadows reaching outward.

Lydia took a breath and she let it go. She paused and played her recording into the air. The call echoed out, lonely amongst the trees. Going still to listen, she stood motionless a long time.

"Are you upset with me, Lydia?"

She turned to face him. "Why are you here, Louis? What are you after? What do you want from me?"

"I told you..."

"...You grew up reading my books..." She shook her head and looked away into the distance. "I know, alright? I know Michael was unfaithful to me. So, what is it—you think he may have been your father? Is that it? And now you're after—what—money?"

Louis was dumbfounded. After a moment, he managed to get out the word, "No."

The distance ahead was blue with snow. Everything was blue or black and the night air was still and sat on Louis's cheeks like cold glass.

He sighed. "When I was a kid... Sometimes it seemed like books were the only friends I had..."

Lydia stared forward. Her jaw was locked and in the moonlight, the sharpness of it looked like something cast in metal. She closed her eyes and said coldly, "So, really, what is this book about?"

"It's about a lose-lose. That's what it's about. I quit my job. I quit, 'cause I couldn't keep it up anymore. I quit because I want to have a family and... I didn't have a father, growing up alright? I don't know what it means to be a father, except that, at the most base level it has to mean being an example, and I can't trick myself into thinking lying fits into that, or hyperbole... Because—you're right—it's garbage, what I was doing... So, I quit. You know what Charlie Puelle says? He says he's sorry I'm leaving. He claps me on the back and tells me, I'm one of the 'good ones.' I don't even know what to do with that." Louis shook his head and looked away for a moment. "When I finish this book, it's gonna fucking ruin him. The closest friend I've ever had. It's gonna bring his empire down. It'll expose him for what he is. A talker. A faker. An opportunist. You see? He wasn't lying to me, when he said he'd take me back. I've been lying to him..."

Lydia was silent.

"I got an advance to write an exposé. That's the book. I'm almost done. But..." He shook his head. "I can't finish." His head kept shaking, as though in a fit. "I thought, if I could find Bigfoot, if we could prove it... Well, who would give a shit about some exposé of the Right World News, then? Really—who would? But... You said it yourself, everything about this is phony..."

"Writer's block? That's all this is about? Jesus, Louis—I've been there. I could give you some advice..."

"It's not about the writing, Lydia. It's about the finishing. I write this book, then what?! What the fuck am I supposed to do then? Who the fuck's gonna hire me then?! I'm losing myself in all this. Who will even want to know me? I'll lose Maria—I feel like I already have... I'll have sold out the only friend who's stuck by me. I'll be alone again, just like when I was a kid. Finishing this book will be the end of me. My fiancé, she doesn't get it. She's never known me without the money. She doesn't know that that part of my life is already over. The Benz, all of it... Once she finds out..." His voice died, his words absorbed entirely by the still coldness of the air.

Lydia nodded and closed her eyes. When she lifted her head, she said, "You'll figure it out."

"That's it? That's your sage advice?"

She shrugged. "What can I tell you? What do you expect from me? I'm at the end of my career, too," she said and let out a sour little laugh and moved on again.

Louis followed. They crossed the source of a brook—a spout of ice jutting from a hillside. Lydia played her recording and the sound carried into the woods.

They stood silent and listened. Then, they moved on again.

After awkwardly crossing over a downed tree (the snowshoes felt very heavy this evening, heavier with each step), Louis said, "Can I ask you something?"

Lydia was silent and so Louis said, "I don't know how you can say you're at the end of your career. You act like it isn't anything at all, everything you've accomplished; everything you've discovered. You found proof, Lydia—actual proof. No one else can say that."

Still facing forward she said, "The Wilton Incident?"

"Of course."

Her voice sounded choked when she said, "Michael took those pictures." She shrugged. The gesture looked like defeat.

"Yeah, I know that. I've read the book."

"He recorded the call." Her voice sounded grave.

"Yeah. Lydia, I know. I've read all your books. I told you that."

"No, Louis. You don't understand. He took the pictures. I never saw anything." She shook the portable speaker dangling in her hand. "He recorded the call. I never even heard it..."

"Lydia..."

"I've never seen anything else; nothing so meaningful that it still sticks with me, nothing so sturdy that it can't be reasoned away. I believed because of him and now... Now, I don't know if I believe anything at all..."

"Why do you think he was unfaithful?"

In the darkness, Lydia pawed at her eyes brusquely with the backside of her glove. "Six month ago. This girl showed up at my door. Around your age. She looked uncomfortable. It kinda fell out of her mouth. I didn't even say a word. I closed the door. I thought it was a con, or something. I'd gotten a lot of weird correspondence in the months after Michael died... I don't know. I figured she was after something... Money... But..."

"My God, Lydia..."

"I never heard from her again. And... I don't know. I don't know why I closed that door. But, I can't convince myself that I wouldn't do the same exact thing all over again. I... I don't know." She wiped at her eyes again.

After she'd cleared her throat and straightened her posture out, she played the recording again, and was about to step forward once more, when a call sounded back.

Straightening to sudden attention, she turned to Louis. His eyes were wide—staring into the distance ahead. After a beat, he turned, and met her gaze. Another call bellowed back—very close, very loud, and they both turned ahead again. When Louis lunged forward, Lydia caught his sleeve in her hand, drawing him to a stop.

"Slowly," she whispered to him.

He nodded, but it was hard moving slowly—the world seemed suddenly too quiet and the whomp and crunch of their snowshoes as singular and concussive as a hammer driving stakes. At the edge of the grove of aspens, the shadows thinned and Louis and Lydia emerged onto the cusp of a treeless slope, stretching away from them. They paused.

Lydia raised up her speaker and played the sound out again.

The noise cut into the distance. A gust of wind rose. Flakes of snow sputtered in the air. The wind died and the world was quiet and still again. Again, she played the call and waited. And then again, before she let the speaker drop in her hand.

"Try again," Louis said, after a moment.

"What's the point, Louis? This is done. This is over with."

"We heard it, Lydia. We both heard it."

"It was probably the wind."

"If anything, it was Clyde," Louis said and Lydia could hear the smirk in his voice. "You said you wanted to put it behind you. So, try it once more and, if nothing happens, we can both let it go."

"Once more?"

He nodded. "Once more."

She raised the speaker again. The sound wound out into the wilderness. A moment passed. Then, louder—loud enough so that it seemed to originate from right beside them—another reply cut through the still air. Lydia's head rose.

Turning to Louis, she threw her arms around him, giving him a sudden, vicious hug. When her hands slipped away, she was running again, hurrying toward the call, half-skiing on her snowshoes down the incline, the snow spilling away ahead of them, hissing and sizzling.

Louis tried to keep up, but couldn't. The toe of his snowshoe caught and he spilled forward, rolling in the snow, snow packing itself into his sleeves and under his collar. The sudden cold got him right back to his feet, and when he rose, he saw that Lydia had fallen as well.

Urgently whispering her name, he hurried forward. By the time he made it to her, she'd sat herself up and was pawing frantically at the snow around her.

"What is it?" he whispered.

"The speaker, I lost it." She kept digging at the snow.

When the call came again, cutting through the distance, Louis took her under her arm and pulled her up. "No time. Let's go."

Lydia nodded and together they slid down the remainder of the hill, where they could hear the noise of the river again. The water was visible now, silhouettes of trees laying starkly against the silver gleam.

In a gap between two trees, the Sasquatch was finally in sight—a bulky black figure framed with silvery-lit water—raising his chin and bellowing into the night.

Lydia and Louis both stopped, dumbfounded.

"My God," Lydia muttered. Her own voice seemed to spur her to action. Digging into her pocket, she fished out her phone. Raising it up, she started filming, and began to advance once more.

Louis started forward as well, keeping just beside her. The Sasquatch didn't seem to notice them. He tilted his chin again and let loose another lonesome cry, his anguished song warbling into the wilderness.

When Lydia, her attention fixed on the luminous image bobbing on the screen of her phone, stumbled, Louis was quick to catch her and steady her. She nodded her thanks and kept onward, her focus never leaving the screen.

They were so close now that, with the zoom at its limit, the Sasquatch filled the screen. And, suddenly, the beast seemed to become aware of them. Turning his back to the river, his eyes

gleamed with moonlight and the giant proportions and awkward arrangement of his body suddenly became clear. Naked
from head to toe and sunk into the snow to his knees, Clyde
stared back at them.

"Oh. You gotta be kidding me," Louis muttered, his shoulders suddenly dropping. "What the hell are you doing, you lu-
natic?" Brokering the distance, Lydia and Louis met Clyde where
he stood, sunk into the snow. Standing atop the snow in his
snowshoes, Louis was taller than the man now, by some inches.

Clyde seemed confused. "Did you not hear the call?"

"Oh, for Christ's sake. That was us, Clyde!"

At Louis's side, Lydia dropped back, sitting down in the
snow, exhausted, numb, vexed.

"You're going to catch hypothermia, you dumb Swede."
Louis thrust out his hand, pointing downriver in the direction of
the derelict camp. "Go put your damned clothes on."

Clyde struggled through the deep snow to approach Louis,
lifting his knees toward his sternum. "I do not know why you
insist on calling me Swede."

"Because that's what you are. Rabbits and raccoons are a
goddamned rodents and you're a goddamned Swede."

The naked giant paused, shaking his head. "No. It is not
true."

"Your name is Fredric Haake. You used to be a real estate
developer in Seattle. You're blonde and you still would be if you
didn't dye your hair."

Clyde looked around and, after a moment, nodded. "Yes. It
is true. I once was Frederic Haake. I was greedy and assembled
much wealth..."

"Jesus," Louis shook his head in a spasm. "Stop talking like
that. That is not who you are."

"...I was shot in the head while on a hunting trip. When I
awoke from my coma, I was no longer the man I had been. That
bullet killed Fredric Haake. I no longer cared for the things that
Fredric Haake cared for. I no longer had use for the things he
had loved. And, the things he loved, no longer had love for me.

The wife I had had, left me. The friends I had had, vanished. My family disappeared. They were no longer my family. I knew I had another family and that that family was waiting for me to come and join them and reaffirm our ancient bond."

"Oh, stop, stop. Just stop. There is no Clyde Whitethunder! That is not a real name. You are not a real..." Louis would have continued, but his voice was suddenly broken off by a shrill call from the wilderness across the river.

They all turned. Louis stared and Lydia stared and Clyde raised his head to the sky and gave out a great, whooping response.

In the uncertain, shifting darkness beyond the river, a figure had emerged from the trees.

Louis's mouth fell open, but clamped shut again when Clyde bolted. Kicking his way through the thigh-deep snow, the man made it to the river and, before he could dive in, the ice beneath him gave out. He plunged into the water, disappearing from sight in an instant. Louis hurried forward. His snowshoes catching, he tumbled. Pushing himself up, he gazed out at the water.

Clyde had surfaced, trailing a long plume of black through the moonlit water.

Clambering up onto the far bank, Clyde's mane seemed to have been washed free of the black dye, although that may just have been the paleness of the moonlight shining in his soaking hair. He stood before the other being, both of them too distant now to clearly make out. Louis stared. Lydia stared, both of them breathless.

Across the river, the two spectral figures clasped hands.

Louis turned to look at Lydia. She was staring, unblinking. When Louis looked back across the river, the figures had already disappeared, submerged in the blackness of the forest.

THE FINAL SLIDE, glowing on the projection screen, showed a pair of tracks in the snow. Side by side, they cut into a vacancy between two enormous Douglas Firs. There, the path ended abruptly.

In the gloom of the dimly lit lecture hall, Lydia's voice squawked over the tinny speakers on either side of the dais, "Was it a wild-man we found evidence of that night? A Bigfoot? Some supernatural entity, beyond our comprehension?

"With the DNA test of the sample we found in the bed of Corey Dibiase's truck coming back inconclusive, it's impossible to say. For me, personally, this case has given hope enough, so that I find that this search, which has spanned my entire career, cannot be said to have ended. Not yet." Closing up her laptop, the image on the projection screen vanished. The breathy humming of the computer's fan died, and silence settled in the room.

A moment later, when the lights came up, Lydia was confronted by the relative emptiness of the auditorium. This space was unnecessary. She could have done her presentation in the closest ladies' room and not felt cramped. She could hear her own breath. She could hear the rustling of the skirts of the woman in the front row as the woman stood and began clapping, turning to those few in their seats, as though to display for them how applause was produced. The others joined in, after a moment. It had started too late and it went on too long, Lydia feeling increasingly awkward.

"Questions?" The woman at the front, with her University lanyard swinging before her bosom, asked the crowd.

A man raised his hand. When Lydia said, 'Yes?' he stood.

"Was Tom Morrow ever found?"

Lydia nodded. "Visiting family in Aurora. We tried to get an interview with him about the creature he caught. He refused to speak with us."

She moved on. A few more questions came in: about process, about her plans for the future... about the Wilton Incident. Questions came from the woman with the lanyard, when the rest of the room ran out.

Then, the questions ended altogether.

Lydia came off the dais to stand by a table mounded with copies of her latest book.

The audience divided itself. More than half moved silently to the exit. The slim remainder met Lydia at the table, while the woman with the lanyard stood aside, watching and smiling, her hands held together, her fingers moving as though she was playing an invisible, inaudible instrument.

Lydia sold three copies of the book and signed them. She signed some older books people had brought along, scrawling her name a few more times.

Those who lined up had stories for her, stories about their own encounters. Stories about relatives and friends and strangers all bound together by similar experience. Every audience member who'd waited to meet Lydia seemed more eager to share their own story than to hear hers. They wanted validation.

They wanted to know that mystery still existed; that the world still contained magic.

When the last of the audience had dwindled away, staring at the hardcover in his hand, the woman with the lanyard came forward to thank Lydia for coming. She offered some reserved compliment on the presentation. She apologized that she couldn't help packing up. She had a bad back. The lanyard swung when she spoke.

"It's okay. I have help coming."

When the door at the back of the room opened, the woman with the lanyard went to intercept the man who entered.

Meeting him halfway up the aisle, the woman insisted, "I'm sorry sir, but the event just ended. You'll have to leave."

Louis smiled. "I'm with Lydia."

Nodding and moving aside, the woman moved to the doorway. Lingering there for a moment, she watched Louis. She watched Lydia greet Louis. Only after they hugged did the woman turn and go out. The feeble boom of the door shutting filled the auditorium and Louis and Lydia were alone.

"How'd it go?"

"Would've been better if I wasn't taking books away."

"You brought too many," he said.

"Yeah. Thanks."

He helped her pack up the rest of her things, the books, the bag, the laptop on the dais.

Outside, the night was cool and damp and the flowers in the beds before the University building nodded in the breeze, perfuming the air.

The parking lot was almost empty and Louis led Lydia to his car where it waited in the golden puddle beneath a streetlamp. The Benz was gone. Traded in two Springs prior for a used mini-van with mismatched running boards, the profit of the sale delivered directly to the publisher to forgive Louis's advance. In the end, he'd gotten to sixty-five thousand words. The publisher wanted changes. Louis resisted. In the end, neither would compromise. Louis was relieved to see the project die.

In the passenger seat, Maria looked up from her book as the pair approached. When they were close, she opened the door and wrestled her way out.

She hugged Lydia first, leaning out over her own belly, and after they'd parted, she asked, "How'd the presentation go?"

"It was fine." Redirecting the conversation to Maria, Lydia said, "Not much longer now. Next month, right?"

"The eleventh, they're saying... Not soon enough. I'm tired of lugging the little gent around. Did Louis tell you, we're going to name him Michael?"

Lydia turned to Louis. "No. He did not."

"So much for the surprise, babe," Louis chided his wife.

They stood in the parking lot, arguing about who'd take the backseat. Maria won. No one alive—man or woman—is wise to argue with an expectant mother. Louis opened the sliding door for her and helped get her comfortable while Lydia climbed into the passenger seat.

The night was quiet, out on the road. Tomorrow would be Easter and it seemed that everyone else in the state of Washington had already arrived where they'd spend the holiday. Everyone but Lydia, and Louis and Maria. And Louis drove them out into the night, already anticipating the scent of the strange, salted tofu loaf which his mother would insist was a ham. He could already hear the noise of the wind, their laughter loud above it.

BRAD RAU has worked as a farmhand, a courier, and in the lumber industry. Currently, he divides his time between writing fiction and working as a production editor in academic textbooks. His previous novel, Caveman at the End of the World, was named one of the "Best Books of 2017" by Indie Reader, was shortlisted for both an Indies Book Award and a Maine Literary Award, and was a Discovery Award winner. He lives in Maine with his wife. You can connect with him at bradrau.com

Apologies/Excuses/Acknowledgments

As someone who passed through a very narrow portion of the Olympic Peninsula on a road trip some years ago, I have taken a number of liberties with the setting of this novel and ask forgiveness of anyone closer to that land and her people than I am.

I have many connections to books. One of those connections is that my grandfather worked in books, creating print plates for illustrations. Many of the books that he worked on are sitting on my bookshelf, and truth is, I like a book with illustrations. I find no clear logic in the fact that a classic like Oscar Wilde's The Picture of Dorian Grey, a book clearly not intended for children, gets pictures and yet modern works like Kazuo Ishiguro's The Buried Giant, a book that begs for illustrations, has none (save a beautifully rendered endpaper). Anyway, my point is, I sometimes like a book with pictures. So, that's what I made.

It must be said, this book would not have been possible without the help and talents of a number of people. Thanks and love to my wife, Morgan, whose support and care have proven boundless. Thanks also to Alex Ortolani, who helped at every stage of writing this book, from the initial idea to the final edit. Thank you to my sister, Rainy and to Elizabeth Cameron, who read early version of the book and provided helpful insights and encouragement. Thanks to my mother, and to Ben and Erin Lutton for their unwavering kindness, support, and perennial help with copyediting. Finally, to you, reader: thank you. If you enjoyed this book, please consider leaving a review of it on amazon or goodreads.

Also available from Brad Rau:

"A FORMIDABLE DEBUT…"
-Kirkus Reviews

Once hailed as a local hero for orchestrating the rescue of two lost tourists, Barry Cook has worked hard to put that reputation to rest. Whether he was ever truly clairvoyant or always just a fraud, now—with every other option exhausted, with his freedom and family home in jeopardy—there's little choice but to return to that old role. Barry knows it's treacherous business. When tampering with the paranormal, the divide between life and death can get confused, and negotiating that line becomes an awkward dance: funny, frightening and affecting.

The Ghost, Josephine
ISBN: 980692490587

2017 DISCOVERY AWARD WINNER

In a nameless city in the near future, Ella Pearson returns home to find her apartment broken into. Tiny, mute and covered in hair, the intruder seems harmless enough but, as the simple nuisance of extracting him from her life turns into an all-consuming battle against a mysterious government agency, it becomes evident that he is only a minor instrument in a much greater conspiracy. As the circumstances enveloping her grow increasingly surreal, Ella's attention turns to her own, murky past where she will find answers to questions so monumental, she never considered that they should be asked.

Caveman at the End of the World
ISBN: 9780692884317

bradrau.com